Lena & Miss Cawkwell

JULIE BOZZA

LIBRAtiger

Published by LIBRAtiger 2026
ISBN: 978-1-925869-42-2

Proofreading: Sue Meadows of No Stone Unturned
Cover image: Photograph by Jez Timms on Unsplash

Table of Contents

Chapter One

Lena Pearce flew along the dirt lane on her bicycle, knowing just what strength was needed to maintain her speed, just how fast she could take that next turn. The air was bracingly fresh in her face, tugging strands of her hair loose as it always did no matter how carefully she pinned it up in the grey light of early morning. She wore trousers, close-fitting and cropped short around her calves so she didn't have to worry about them catching in the chain. There were still eyes in the village that looked askance at this despite her boots and socks demurely covering her ankles. Lena grinned to remember old Mrs Bailey staring at her with a thrill of disapproval only yesterday – as if she hadn't had months to get used to Lena doing this work and dressing accordingly. As if she hadn't known the Pearce family's tendency towards contrariness all the days of her life.

The woods on Lena's left veered towards the road as she sped past, thickened, loomed and then leapt across it with overarching branches. Lena coasted through the tunnel of green shade, and then followed the road around the curve, steering with little more than a perfectly judged lean to the left. Then she stood on the pedals to power down the last straight and back into the sunshine, before taking a sharp turn down a side road and at last arriving at Amy's gate.

Lena slid off the bicycle and propped it

against the fence, then hefted the satchel out of the bicycle's basket. As she walked along the path up to the front door, Lena reached into the satchel for the letter, and held it up between two fingers as she knocked. A smile full of promise came naturally to her lips as she heard footfalls coming down the hall, glimpsed movement through the window with its lace curtains. Lena had been happy to find a letter addressed to *Mrs J. Martin* in the sack of mail that morning, and the handwriting and return address meant it wasn't from Amy's husband, who was off fighting the Kaiser. It had been a few days since Lena had seen Amy, and that was far too long...

"Good morning, Lena," said Amy with a sweet though rather distracted smile. "I haven't seen you for a while!" Instead of reaching to take the letter, she stepped back a little – and that was invitation, or at least consent. Lena stepped over the threshold. "Why is it that laundry seems never-ending?" Amy asked over her shoulder as she led Lena through to the kitchen. Amy cast a whimsical gesture in the direction of the washhouse in the back garden, but Lena wasn't really paying attention. Instead, Lena glanced around looking for the children, but decided they must be at school; Amy wouldn't have let her in otherwise. "You'd think that at some point all the clothes would be clean. But no, you turn around and there's always more to be done." As Amy spoke, she topped the kettle up with water from the bucket, and set it on the hottest part of the range, apparently assuming that Lena would stay for a cup of tea.

Lena leaned against the table, simply

enjoying the sight of her. Amy's womanly figure wasn't quite so plump as it had been before the war, but it still curved deliciously. Her red hair used to be long and always kept under some semblance of control in a bun at her nape. It had been almost a year since Amy had cut it short, and now curls bobbed about her pretty face. Other than being about the same height, they were complete opposites, Lena and Amy: Lena was a slim, tough tomboy with a mess of straight dark hair, and she knew there was nothing more than pleasant about her.

"Hhhmmm?" prompted Amy, wanting a response.

Ah yes, the laundry. "The only way you could make sure that all the clothes were clean..." said Lena, stalking towards her, "would be to do the laundry naked."

"Oh!" Amy laughed, and she blushed a little with her hand to her mouth.

Lena dropped to her knees, and pressed her face to Amy's thighs, feeling the slight warmth of flesh even though the layers of cotton, while her hands slipped under the hem of Amy's skirt and shaped themselves to her knees and then slid up and under her slip and further up...

"Oh!" said Amy again. She always sounded surprised, as if Lena didn't do this every time she was invited in, as if Amy wasn't the prettiest thing in the county, as if a woman wouldn't ever find herself doing the laundry one moment and being seduced the next, and in bright daylight, too.

Carefully Lena snared fingers in Amy's

knickers, and drew them slowly down, listening to Amy's breath which was already panting in anticipation. When Lena's hands slid up again, she bundled the skirt as she went – and Lena followed, kneeling up taller, until at last she could apply her tongue where it would do the most good.

"Oh..." moaned Amy, grasping at the back of a chair for support, arching delightfully and pushing forward. "Oh, Lena, Lena, you're spoiling me, you're ruining me..."

Lena paused and looked up with a quizzical brow.

Amy laughed breathlessly – and though a shade of doubt crossed her lovely face, she smiled, and shook it off. "But please don't stop."

Lena grinned, and continued her work.

"You're absolutely wicked," said Emily, slipping down further on the sofa and propping both bare feet on the shabby old pouffe. Her long dark hair cascaded over the back of the sofa and disappeared from view. Lena's fingers twitched; she always wanted to plait it, as she'd used to do when they were girls. And then she wanted to mess it up again...

"While the men are away, Lena will play."

Emily was unimpressed, of course, but her smile remained fond and her gaze remained languid. "I suppose I shouldn't be thinking 'Poor Amy', though, should I?"

"It's not as if she even resists," Lena replied, "let alone fights me off. And it would take a saint to resist her. She's so adorable! She always was."

Emily took a long drag on the hand-rolled cigarette and passed it back. "You've had quite a morning, then."

"I have," Lena agreed, glancing a grin Emily's way. "Eva Rowan had a couple of letters, too."

Emily laughed as if she shouldn't be surprised any more. "Delivered personally, I take it."

"Of course! It's all part of the service."

"I thought you didn't even *like* Eva. We were never friends with her at school."

Lena shrugged. "I like her well enough," she said in tones that didn't invite a response.

In the comfortable silence, Lena huffed on the very last scrap of the cigarette, pinching it between finger and thumb until the embers finally drew too close to bear. She stubbed out the little that remained – and then when Emily lifted an arm towards her, Lena happily went to cosy up beside her. She curled in further, and pushed her feet in their socks – the boots having already been abandoned – next to Emily's, before running the arch of a foot up the long curve of Emily's calf. Lena sighed. "What sort of letter will it take..." she mused, "for you to finally accept a personal delivery?"

"Oh, darling," came the brisk response, "we've been friends for *ever*. As good as *sisters*. Doesn't that disqualify me?"

"No." Lena looked up from Emily's shoulder, let her gaze roam over that face – still so pretty despite being so utterly familiar – and favoured Emily with a wistful look.

"I'm your best friend, and I will be till the day I die. The rest," Emily added, in somewhat less high-flown tones, "you get plenty of elsewhere."

"Oh, darling..." Lena echoed with a sigh.

Someone had finally moved into the house at Fields Corner that had been empty for so long, but it was a week or so before Lena had any mail to deliver. Eventually a letter arrived, addressed to *Miss Cawkwell*. A pity the newcomer was a Miss rather than a Mrs, but then so many good things were in short supply these days. Lena mentally revised her route, and rode down there in a state of some curiosity.

She took it easier than her usual pace, stretching out the anticipation. Fresh breezes buffeted the unusually long grass in the fields, creating waves of silver amid the green. An occasional unfortunate scent added a discordant note, but Lena shrugged this off. Smells were hardly unexpected in the heart of farmland and countryside! Everything felt delightfully unsettled.

As Lena neared the bend of the road that would take her to the house, she slowed further – not because the bend was an uncompromising ninety degrees, but because Lena glimpsed movement through the hedgerows, and wanted to scout the lie of the land. She came to a gentle halt, balanced lightly with the ball of one foot on the ground, and peered around the end of the hedge.

A woman, presumably Miss Cawkwell, was standing in the overgrown front garden, staring in perplexity at a nanny goat who was cheerfully – one might even say cheekily – munching on weeds. The goat tore off another bunch and lifted her head to placidly meet Miss Cawkwell's gaze, stalks sticking out of her mouth in every direction, with yellow flowers bobbing at the end of each.

Miss Cawkwell took a step towards the goat; the goat took a jaunty step back. Miss Cawkwell edged to her left as if considering trying to circle around; the goat danced to her right. Lena's smile quirked as she reflected that the goat was the more graceful of the pair. Miss Cawkwell stalled again, and put her hands on her hips – apparently in confusion rather than consternation. Confusion or not, though, the young woman was not backing down.

Lena took in the sight of Miss Cawkwell, though of course she still suffered the disadvantage of being a Miss. There were so many reasons for Lena to prefer women with other commitments. Apart from which, Miss Cawkwell was too tall, all long limbs and angles, as if she would never quite grow out of the colt stage. Her hair was flat and mousy brown, clumsily cut in a short bob, with a couple of pins failing in their task of fixing back the longer strands. She wore a shapeless gingham dress, with a long apron tied over it, and a pair of overly practical shoes. Miss Cawkwell was, in sum, not the sort to entice interest. Though Lena couldn't help but notice that Miss Cawkwell had a long lovely neck, a pale shapely column that provided her only element of elegance.

Finally, several moments later, Lena pushed off and coasted the bicycle to the front gate. "Good morning!" she called.

Miss Cawkwell looked around distractedly, saw Lena – saw the satchel, and the letter in Lena's hand. "Good morning," she replied, in an appropriately rough voice. She strode over to the gate, not neglecting to swing a hand against a nettle on her way, and almost trip over a tuft of grass. There was already a nettle rash running up the tender side of one forearm. "Are you the postman, then?"

Lena grinned. "I am," she replied, handing over the letter. "I used to help my Uncle Bill anyway, so when he enlisted I took on the job."

Miss Cawkwell nodded. After giving the letter a cursory look, she tucked it unopened into a pocket.

Lena found she wasn't ready to be dismissed yet, but Miss Cawkwell was no doubt as aware as Lena was of the date that the call for volunteers went out: 11 August 1914, just over ten months ago. The day when everything changed. Instead, Lena tipped her chin towards the goat. "I see you have the gardener in, helping you clear the weeds."

That drew a laugh from Miss Cawkwell. It was an odd kind of laugh, beginning with a honking snort and ending up as a peal of bells. After a moment, Miss Cawkwell said, "My intention is to milk her."

"She's not cooperating?"

"And I don't understand why. I went to fetch

her yesterday evening from Mrs Doherty. Being away from her kids overnight – Well," Miss Cawkwell concluded with a slight hint of confusion at this intimate subject, "she's supposed to welcome the milking."

"Yet she'd rather eat weeds."

Miss Cawkwell smiled a little, ducking her head shyly. "Perhaps she's naturally mischievous."

"Stubborn," Lena countered, able for the moment to gaze her fill at Miss Cawkwell's lovely neck. When Miss Cawkwell looked up again, Lena got off the bicycle and propped it against the thick hedge which was haphazardly sprouting new growth. "Let's see if we can't outwit her. Lena Pearce," she introduced herself, holding out her hand.

"Sylvie Cawkwell," Miss Cawkwell responded, going to open the gate, then shaking Lena's hand instead, then barking her shin on the gate as it belatedly swung free. Sylvie grimaced – but not heatedly – as if she were used to this sort of thing.

The two of them strolled with a fair pretence of nonchalance towards the goat – who considered them with a bright eye while still munching away – and then as they finally drew near, she skittered off out of reach. This despite the obvious fact that her udder was full.

"I don't think she'll mind very much if we trick her into it," Lena said. "I think she'll be grateful."

"She'll forgive me, then? She'll let me milk her again? My landlady – of course you'd know her – Mrs Doherty said I could have her every other day."

"Yes, I think she'll forgive you. The goat, that is."

"Ideas?" asked Miss Cawkwell.

"Well…" Lena considered for a moment. "You're the one who needs to make friends with her. Why don't you gather up a large bouquet of those yellow flowers she likes so much, and tempt her hither – while I circle around behind, and give her a push in the right direction."

Miss Cawkwell looked at Lena with frank admiration. "A master strategist."

She smiled in response, unaccountably bashful. "Let's see if it works first!"

By the time Miss Cawkwell had gathered an armful of flowers, Lena had managed to nonchalantly sneak around behind the goat. With a nod they each indicated they were ready – and Miss Cawkwell brandished the flowers at the goat while Lena grabbed the goat's hips and shoved. The goat obligingly took a step or two forward and stretched in hope of a mouthful of flowers. Miss Cawkwell stepped back at just the right moment, the goat took another step, and they all three progressed from there in fits and starts.

"Does she have a name?" Lena asked, aware of her breath beginning to pant from the effort.

"Christabel."

Lena let out a laugh. "Ha! A pretty name for such a stubborn thing. What was Mrs Doherty thinking?"

"I don't know –" As Miss Cawkwell leant

down to gather more of the weeds while still backing away, she abruptly overbalanced and landed on her rear. She didn't even take a moment to huff a breath before scrambling back up to her feet, ungainly and yet endearing in her determination.

"Are you all right?" Lena asked.

"Yes, thank you. Come on, Christabel..."

"Not bruised?" Lena cast an eye towards the rounded curve that could just be discerned under the loosely hung gingham.

"Oh! Yes, probably! Never mind." Miss Cawkwell gathered more of the flowers as she went, no doubt so as not to leave any as distractions in the goat's path.

Lena smiled at her, and gave Christabel another shove. "Where are we heading?"

Miss Cawkwell gestured behind her. "There's a shelf for her to stand on just inside the shed." This was announced with rather a lack of authority, so Lena concluded she was needed for the duration. She was torn between silently castigating Mrs Doherty for leaving Miss Cawkwell to manage things alone, and quietly singing her thanks. Lena was having fun.

Once they were out of the old flower beds, Christabel stopped being so difficult. Soon she was daintily stepping up the slope that led to the milking shelf, eagerly pursuing the bunch of weeds that Miss Cawkwell placed in the feeder.

"Shall I show you...?" Lena offered.

"Please," said Miss Cawkwell.

So Lena helped Miss Cawkwell add grain to

the feeder, then wash Christabel's udder, and inspect a cup's worth of milk before placing the bucket beneath the goat and settling into the task. Lena showed her where to sit, and in what posture, and how to avoid Christabel kicking at her in irritation. She helped guide Miss Cawkwell's hands on Christabel's teats, encouraged her towards a rippling rhythm of fingers. Miss Cawkwell soon had the idea of it, even if her fingers wouldn't quite coordinate. All the while, the two women and the goat were close and warm and... and Lena at least was feeling a little inappropriate. Judging by Miss Cawkwell's slight blush, there was a chance that she felt somewhat the same way, even if it were only modesty that heightened her colour rather than desire.

Once the process was over and poor Christabel's udder was looking suitably shrivelled, Lena carefully set the bucket of milk out of the way, and then showed Miss Cawkwell how to massage the udder and clean the teats. Christabel seemed satisfied to the point of smugness, munching away on the grain and what was left of the flowers.

"Right," Lena finally announced. "I think we're done."

"Thank you," said Miss Cawkwell. Her cheeks were red and her demeanour was flustered, but her neck remained cool and pale and elegant. Miss Cawkwell lifted a hand to try to brush back the longer strands of her hair which had come loose. "I'll walk her back to Mrs Doherty."

"Do you have a lead?"

"Oh. Yes." Miss Cawkwell went to fetch it,

and by luck managed to fasten it to Christabel's collar just before the goat decided to leap down to the ground – stepping on Miss Cawkwell's foot in the process, though it was Christabel who bleated a protest.

"Would you like company for the walk?" Lena cleared her throat. "Just in case she gets stubborn again."

"Oh, no. No, thank you. You've helped me so much already, Miss Pearce."

"Lena."

"Lena." Miss Cawkwell blushed even harder. "I'm sure you have the rest of your round to finish."

"Well..." Should Lena confess that she'd left Miss Cawkwell until last? Perhaps not.

"Thank you. I would have been quite lost without you."

"Oh, you're so –" *lovely*. "Welcome." Lena smiled. "You're so very welcome. Sylvie."

They accompanied each other and Christabel to the front gate, navigated this obstacle with difficulty, and then suffered through clumsy farewells – not helped by Christabel circling them and winding the lead around their knees. At last Lena managed to disengage, and climbed onto her bicycle so that she could escape down the road in an ecstatic kind of agony.

"If only she weren't a Miss!"

Emily laughed, recumbent on the sofa as usual, with her bare feet on the pouffe. Lena was aware of Emily watching her as she paced back and forth, too skittish to settle. Emily was about to speak, then seemed to change her mind. When Lena turned again to pace towards her, Emily remarked, "It's true, my darling, she doesn't seem at all your type."

"Single."

"And not pretty!"

Lena stopped, and ran wondering fingers across her own throat, remembering... "She has the most elegant neck you will ever see."

"Ah..." Emily sounded sceptical.

Lena laughed, and faced her best friend. "Am I so shallow, then?"

"Yes, my dear, I'm afraid that you are."

She laughed again, and wandered off, this time to gaze sightlessly through the window into Emily's back garden. "But she was so... Sylvie was so..."

"First names already, is it? Not 'Miss Cawkwell'?"

"She was so... tenacious."

"Tenacious!" Emily pushed up to sit a little straighter. "And that rates more than pretty now, does it?"

Lena was looking at neat rows of fulsome cabbages, and remembering a mess of nettles, and weeds with yellow flowers. Remembering Sylvie facing down the placidly mischievous Christabel. Lena felt she had known from the start who would win the confrontation. "It's as if she faces challenge after challenge every day of her life, and she never lets it defeat her."

Emily lifted her brows.

"All right, maybe some of those challenges are just bruises or tripping over a tussock or having to wear a ghastly gingham dress... but she sails smoothly on. Yes!" Lena cried, the correct simile finally occurring to her. "She's like an ugly duckling who hasn't quite transformed yet into a beautiful swan. She has the neck, though. She really does have the loveliest long pale neck. And maybe none of the rest of her will ever quite catch up – but she has the attitude, too. She sails on through all the things that the world throws at her, and she remains her own true self."

When Lena got to the end of that, she pushed her hands into her trouser pockets and turned to face Emily with at least a pretence of defiance.

Emily stared back at her, eyes wide as if she were stunned. "Well," she said eventually. "Perhaps it's just as well that she's a Miss."

"Why?" asked Lena. "So I won't attempt her seduction?"

"No, so that you can let her seduce you right back."

Lena coasted along the lane on her bicycle, knowing just when to push the pedals through a half-turn to maintain her speed. The air was warmer today, though still fresh against her face as she glided past hedgerows and transformed the road's turns into elegant curves. She drew near the woods and then slipped silently through the living cathedral of arched branches, swept to the left, eased into the side road, and finally drew up to stop at Amy's gate.

Lena was smiling, and keen to see Amy – but even Lena knew that her smile was gentler, and her eagerness had changed. Which was just as well, because when Amy answered the front door, she was shining with joy. For a moment Lena's heart thudded in an answering song, an honest panic – and in the next breath she realised that of course Amy's joy had nothing at all to do with her.

"Oh, Lena, Lena," Amy murmured, slipping onto the front step and closing the door behind her. They were standing so very close to each other, and yet Lena knew that last inch of air between them would never be crossed again. "He's come home. My Joe's come home."

Lena quirked a grin in genuine satisfaction. "That's marvellous, Amy. That's really wonderful."

"It is, isn't it?" Amy was almost breathless with happiness. Lena had never seen her quite like it. "And he's all right – there's some treatment he must continue with, rehabilitation, he won't tell me the details – but even once his leave finishes, he'll be serving in England now. They won't send him overseas again. He'll be here, he won't come to any more harm. Or no more than the rest of us."

"That really is wonderful, Amy."

"I know. It really is." But then Amy paused, and considered Lena for a long moment. "I'm sorry, Lena."

"You have nothing to be sorry about," Lena protested.

"Are you all right, though? You look... different."

"Do I?" Lena dropped her gaze and turned

away a little to ponder that. A long pale elegant neck came to mind, along with the nettle rash on a tender forearm as Miss Cawkwell patiently pushed back a strand of mousy brown hair. "Maybe I am. But don't worry, my darling. It's not about you."

"No?" Amy sounded relieved, and just the smallest bit disappointed.

Lena smiled at her. "I'm so happy for you and Joe, Amy." She belatedly handed over the letters. "Back to regular deliveries from now on, I swear."

Amy took the letters, and slipped her hand around the doorknob. But before turning it, she looked at Lena and her smile turned mischievous as she whispered, "I want to say thank you, Lena."

Lena laughed, and shook her head in disbelief while stepping onto the path and slowly backing away. "I have to go. Deliveries to make!"

"Have fun!" cried Amy.

"Did you know," Lena asked, pausing for a moment at the gate, "that a Miss Cawkwell has moved into Fields Corner?"

Chapter Two

"Good," Eva Rowan said brusquely when she opened her front door to find Lena on the doorstep. "Come," she added, stepping aside and showing no interest in the two letters Lena held. "I have news."

Lena walked in and placed the letters on the hallstand, before casting a curious look around. Eva took her by the hand, and began in her usual no-nonsense way leading Lena down the hallway to the bedroom. But on the way, Lena spied through a doorway a number of textbooks, notepads and pens spread across the dining table. "Are you studying chemistry again?" she asked. "Did you decide to try for Cambridge after all? Or was it Oxford...?" Such distinctions meant little to Lena, but she knew that wasn't the case for Eva. "That's wonderful, either way!"

"No." Eva's house was only small – a cottage, really, though modern. It was plain that Eva had never planned to have children, there just wasn't the space here for more than two people – and given that Eva's husband had been missing since the very earliest days of the war, almost before there was any action in which to go missing, perhaps that was just as well.

They were already walking into the bedroom, in which the curtains were drawn unseasonably early, so Lena shook off the gloomy reflections. It was barely afternoon, and obviously Eva had been expecting her.

As Eva drew Lena into her arms, she repeated, "No. I have work to do." Eva considered Lena for a long moment, her eerily pale blue eyes as sharp as ever despite the minimal makeup she now wore. Her eye shadow used to be dark and dramatic, even on ordinary days, before the war had begun to narrow everyone's priorities. Eva was as beautiful as an enchantress on a stage. But even so, Lena found herself pondering, not even Eva had a neck as elegant as Miss Cawkwell's...

Lena sighed.

As if in response, Eva continued, "I'll be out five, sometimes six days a week. You'll have to visit in the evenings instead." And Eva's arms tightened around her as she pressed her mouth to Lena's.

The two of them were just of a height for their nipples to jostle together, at which a jangle of excitement danced through Lena. Nevertheless, she pulled back a little to say, "I only make deliveries in the morning."

Eva pouted sensually. "But of course you'll make an exception for your favourite correspondent...?"

Despite herself, a laugh burst out of Lena at this absurdity – and, for the briefest and most unexpected of moments, Eva looked startled, before her customary sardonic expression reasserted itself. Lena lifted a hand to stroke the fall of Eva's thick glossy black hair, which was probably all the apology Eva wanted or needed, and then Lena pushed in again to return Eva's kiss.

Soon they were in their usual configuration. Lena was on her back on the bed, with her trousers undone and her pants pushed just low enough for Eva to be thrusting two fingers into her, hard and relentless, with the ball of her thumb rubbing up against her lips, sending vibrations through her nub. Eva was kneeling beside her, securing her balance with her free hand grasping the bedhead, and Lena was returning the favour exactly, with Eva's narrow skirt and petticoat hiked up her thighs.

It was over fast, as always. They had learned, they had perfected their technique, and Eva seemed as interested in efficiency in this as in all else. Lena had no complaints to make. When she wanted savoury, after all, she went elsewhere, and when she wanted sweet, she went to... No, not Amy. Not anymore.

Lena groaned at the thought, and tensed up around Eva's hand, feeling another shock of sensation jolt through her. She curled up while Eva quieted her touch, teasing more quakes from her – until enough was enough, and Lena stilled, and then carefully withdrew her own hand.

Eva stretched out to lie beside her, rolling her shoulders as if resettling herself. They weren't touching now, but still there was a sense of camaraderie between them. A comfortable silence.

Eventually, Lena asked, "What sort of work? Something scientific?" Eva had always been good at that at school.

Eva threw her a wink and a grin. "I can't say."

"War work, then," Lena concluded.

The grin turned wry, and Eva didn't answer. Her eyes were shining, though, and Lena knew that wasn't entirely due to herself or their recent activities.

"That's good," Lena continued as she climbed out of bed and put her clothes to rights. "Your mind is as fabulous as the rest of you," she said, casting an appreciative eye down Eva's gorgeous hourglass form. "You deserve the chance to use it."

An unusually affectionate smile curved Eva's lips. "Thank you, Lena."

There was no sign she was going to move any time soon, so Lena decided to show herself out. "I have to go!" she called back over her shoulder as she headed down the hall.

"Come back soon," Eva called after her. "One evening next week!"

Laughing fondly, Lena headed out.

Lena wheeled her bicycle round to the back of her family home, propped it against the wall, and walked in through the back door. She was about to call a greeting to her mother, but shut her mouth again when she heard the quiet grumble of a conversation coming from the direction of the shop at the front of the house. There had always been customers who would not and could not be pleased, of course, but the war had exacerbated that.

Content to avoid the disagreement for now, Lena unlocked the small back room from which they ran the Post Office, and stepped inside. It only took a moment or two to hang her empty satchel on its accustomed hook, and check that there had been no extra deliveries of mail since the regular morning delivery, no telegrams waiting. Any day without telegrams was a good day.

When Lena emerged again, the conversation was still rumbling along, so letting out a sigh she headed into the shop. Not that her mum, Ruth, would need reinforcements, but moral support was always welcome.

Lena was unsurprised to find that it was Mrs Makepeace confronting Ruth across the counter. Today the subject was sugar. "I'm sure you have supplies of the nicer kind of sugar," Mrs Makepeace was insisting. "How could we possibly have run out so soon?"

"The beet sugar came from Austria," Ruth explained for what sounded like the umpteenth time. "After almost a year of war with Germany, you can hardly expect it to still be available."

Mrs Makepeace's expression turned sly. "I'm sure, Mrs Pearce, that you have some put by for... friends." As if realising that was two or three steps too far, she added quickly, "I mean, for the more *discerning* kind of customer."

Lena's hackles were bristling over this accusation, but Ruth quieted her with a gentle hand on her arm, and replied with no hint of indignation, "We are all using cane sugar now, Mrs Makepeace, and have been for some weeks."

"Really," Mrs Makepeace responded in sceptical tones.

"The canes are shipped from South America, so at least we won't need to worry about running short – even if it's not quite to your taste."

Mrs Makepeace sniffed, and at last handed over a coin to pay for the modest bag of sugar sitting on the counter.

"Thank you, Mrs Makepeace," Ruth said as she returned the woman's change. "Good day."

Another sniff, and then a disapproving glance at Lena, standing there at her mother's shoulder, dressed so very improperly in trousers. Mrs Makepeace picked up the sugar and turned to go – but then turned back round again. "*You* would know," she said to Lena, "now that you're filling in for your uncle."

Lena responded with a noncommittal murmur.

Mrs Makepeace was not discouraged. "Mrs Doherty told me that Fields Corner has been let – to a Miss Cawkwell from London. And she's living there all on her own!"

Lena could feel herself brighten and swell with interest. She hadn't known about London. But, still. It wasn't only that Lena was constitutionally wary of gossip, it was also that Post Office business wasn't to be shared with all and sundry.

"Where are her family, do you know?" Mrs Makepeace continued. "That's a Yorkshire name. Why didn't she go home to Yorkshire?"

"I'm sure we don't have the first idea," Ruth said briskly, cutting off any further enquiries.

"I wouldn't tell you if I *did* know," Lena added for good measure – earning herself glances of mild reproval from her mother and high dudgeon from their customer.

"Well! Good day, Mrs Pearce," Mrs

Makepeace said, turning away and pointedly excluding Lena from her farewell. A moment later the bell tinkled as Mrs Makepeace left, firmly closing the door behind her.

A moment's silence grew, and eventually Lena offered her mother a contrite look.

Ruth seemed to realise that Lena didn't feel particularly apologetic, and apparently Ruth didn't really expect her to, either. "If you're done with the post for the morning," Ruth said, "you can find me the rice in the storeroom. Everything's turned topsy-turvy in there!"

"Yes, Mum," Lena said dutifully. But she paused to press an affectionate kiss to Ruth's temple before heading for the stores, and Ruth turned away with a contented smile.

Lena didn't have any post to deliver to Miss Cawkwell, but she had been keeping track of the days, and she assumed that Christabel would be at Fields Corner for milking. That was enough of an excuse to ride there late that morning, once her satchel was empty.

When she arrived, Lena found Miss Cawkwell backing steadily across the garden, enticing Christabel to follow her by proffering a bunch of the yellow-flowered weeds in her direction. The goat followed her readily enough, with little more than a pretence of reluctance. As the pair neared the shed, Lena let herself in through the gate and lifted a hand in greeting. Miss Cawkwell smiled to see her, and returned the gesture – knocking the tip of her elbow against the shed door as she backed in. Lena's eyes watered in sympathy, but Miss Cawkwell bore it stoically.

Christabel was already in place on the milking shelf when Lena finally followed them in, and was too busy munching away at the flower-decorated grain in her feeder to pay Lena any mind. Miss Cawkwell was still smiling, though, which seemed to indicate she was happy to see her. "Good morning, Miss Pearce," she said.

"How d'you do, Miss Cawkwell?" Lena responded, smiling helplessly as if she were a mirror for this woman's emotions.

Miss Cawkwell had placed the bucket under Christabel, and was settling herself on the stool when she turned back towards Lena, almost losing her balance as she did so. "I'm very well, thank you. I hope you can say the same?"

Lena just nodded, and then watched as Miss Cawkwell began milking Christabel. The goat flicked an ear back, but was otherwise undisturbed. Lena cleared her throat. "Seems the two of you are getting used to each other now."

"Yes, though I couldn't have got her started without your help that first day."

A puff of breath was meant to convey that it was nothing. Though Lena wondered if Miss Cawkwell could read her physical shorthand. Almost everyone else in the village had had years to become familiar with it.

"You were right, of course," Miss Cawkwell continued. "Christabel is grateful to be milked. It was just a matter of convincing her that I was the woman for the job."

"Indeed."

Miss Cawkwell was silent for a long moment. The milk squirted into the bucket strongly but with a complete lack of rhythm. "I'm afraid I still need to work on the knack of rippling my fingers down her teats without tugging at her. Christabel rarely grumbles, but I'm not the most coordinated person in the world."

Lena tried to smother a laugh at this understatement, and was unsuccessful. Luckily, Miss Cawkwell took no offence at this, and instead threw an amused glance over her shoulder. Lena approached, and crouched by Miss Cawkwell to see if she could offer any advice. "All right... you're probably aware you're not rippling in order. From the top finger to the bottom, and from the top to the bottom again." Really, there was no rhyme or reason to how Miss Cawkwell was working Christabel's teats. It was oddly mesmerising! Lena cleared her throat again. "Not that you're not getting a pretty good stream of milk anyway."

"There are *some* things," Miss Cawkwell muttered in defiance, "at which my fingers are surprisingly competent."

Lena turned her head in surprise, and found herself almost cheek to cheek with Miss Cawkwell, with the heat from Christabel and the scent of the milk and the warmth of Miss Cawkwell's blush making Lena feel flushed.

A moment passed.

"*Knitting*, for instance," Miss Cawkwell continued with a tartness that might be due to any number of circumstances.

A laugh hooted out of her, and Lena collapsed back to sit on the straw-covered floor of the shed.

She settled there to keep Miss Cawkwell company until her task was done, and provided what encouragement she could for Miss Cawkwell's efforts to improve her milking technique. Once Christabel was as good as empty, the two women cleaned her up and set her free.

Miss Cawkwell lifted the bucket of milk, and asked, "Would you care to come in for a cup of tea, Miss Pearce?"

Lena's heart thudded in her chest. "I will if you call me Lena."

"I will if you'll call me Sylvie."

"Then, thank you, Sylvie. I'd love a cup of tea."

Miss Cawkwell – Sylvie – smiled, and led the way into the house through the back door.

Lena had never visited Fields Corner before, so looked about her curiously, though there was nothing really unexpected in this farmhouse built perhaps fifty years ago. Sylvie took the fresh milk into the larder to keep it cool, and came out again to stoke the fire in the modest stove and top up the kettle with water. One large spoonful of tea leaves was carefully measured and dropped into the teapot. And then Sylvie settled in to wait for the water to boil, with one hip propped against the stone worktop.

A moment slipped by, and then Sylvie announced, "I've made some cheese, if you'd care to take some home with you. Not that there's very much, so if you have a large family –"

"It's just me and Mum at home, since Uncle Bill joined up. But... you made cheese from the goat's milk?"

"Yes. I know it's not to everyone's taste. Some find it hard to digest."

"I've never had any before," Lena said. "I don't mean to sound ungrateful, but it doesn't have a great reputation!"

Sylvie nodded, unoffended. "I realise that's the common reaction, but it's cows' milk that disagrees with me. Which is why I asked Mrs Doherty if I could have the use of Christabel."

Lena was curious to know what Mrs Doherty asked for in return, but managed to suppress the question. "If you're willing to share a little of the cheese, I'm sure we'd both like to try it. And next time you come to the shop – my Mum runs the grocer's in the village – you must have something in kind."

"Oh, that's not necessary, Lena, with all the help you've already given me. I appreciate the thought, though."

At last the kettle was simmering, so Sylvie turned away. Soon she was ready with the full teapot, cups, saucers, spoons and a sugar bowl on a tray. "I'm sorry, I hope you don't mind taking your tea black. Even I don't like goats' milk in tea, and I wasn't expecting visitors."

"I've developed a taste for black tea," Lena assured her. The war seemed to have pared things back to the essentials. For now, at least, that had the interest of novelty.

"Thank you," Sylvie replied. "Shall we go through to the front room?"

There were two mismatched armchairs in there, with a rickety table between. Lena looked around curiously again, wondering at the sparse possessions. It was as if Sylvie had brought hardly anything with her, and was making do with what little furniture and fittings had been left behind at Fields Corner. Given the house had been sitting empty for some while, Lena didn't like to think about the state it was all in. Still, at least the house didn't feel damp, so hopefully things had been preserved well enough, and it seemed clear that Sylvie must have at least done some serious cleaning and dusting.

When Sylvie looked up from pouring the tea, Lena felt sure she'd been caught being nosy – and so blurted out the first question that occurred to her. "Have you visited the shop yet? I'm never there in the mornings now, with my delivery run. You might have already met Mum."

"I haven't yet, but I was planning to come in over the next day or two. I managed to bring some supplies with me from London, and the vegetable garden here is horribly overgrown but there are treasures to be found there if you know where to look."

Lena grinned at her. Imagine making grubbing around for vegetables sound like an adventure! But the bigger adventure was surely "London...?"

"Yes." Sylvie looked away, self-conscious at

first, then turning thoughtful – and then troubled. She lifted her free hand to her sternum, almost as if searching for something. Whatever it was, it was missing.

Eventually Sylvie glanced up from her reverie with a smile, seeming almost unaware of the quiet moments that had passed. "London," she confirmed.

Lena was feeling horribly curious. "Do you have family there?"

"Family? No."

It wasn't any of Lena's business, really. No more than it was Mrs Makepeace's. But she couldn't resist prompting, "Do you have family here, then?"

"No."

"What brought you here?"

Sylvie considered Lena closely for a moment, with a glint in her eyes as intelligent as Eva's. "Prevailing winds," she replied, though in amused tones rather than sarcastic. "The availability of the house, which I heard about from friends of... friends of an acquaintance. I might have landed anywhere there was a place for me!" Sylvie left a beat, and then asked in wry tones, "Why do you ask, Lena? Are people gossiping?"

Lena flushed a little, not liking to be implicated in such goings-on, but feeling guilty nevertheless. "I'm sorry. We don't get many new people here – We didn't even before the war. I suppose it's not unexpected that people are curious." She admitted, "I'm curious, too!"

Sylvie simply looked back at Lena, without a shred of defensiveness about her. "*You're* not suspicious of me, though, are you?" And apparently this didn't require an answer, because Sylvie smoothly continued, "Speaking of knitting –"

'*Were we? Oh, yes!*' Lena vaguely remembered a brief mention, anyway.

"Is there a local chapter of the Needlework Guild here?"

"The...?"

"The Needlework Guild, organised by the Red Cross Society." Miss Cawkwell obviously realised Lena needed a fuller explanation. "Women sew and knit garments for the servicemen, on the Front as well as those in hospital."

"Ah! I think there is," Lena said. "At least, I know who to ask."

"Thank you. If you could let them know – and if I'm welcome, of course – I'd be delighted to join."

Lena nodded. "Of course." And then they sat there together, drinking their tea. Silent, despite the fact that Lena was as turbulent with questions as ever.

When Lena got home that afternoon, she was delighted to find Amy in the shop across the counter from her mother – pretty Amy with her bobbed red hair and her infectious smile. "Good afternoon, Mrs Martin," said Lena, slipping an affectionate arm around Ruth's waist, seeing as she mustn't embrace Amy now.

"Good afternoon, Miss Pearce," Amy replied with a mischievous twinkle. "I hope you're well."

"Well enough! And you?"

"We're all well, thank you, Miss Pearce – though I have to admit it sometimes seems a mixed blessing these days, to have a family with three such healthy appetites."

Ruth said, "I'm sure you look after them splendidly, Amy, and I trust that you take care of yourself just as splendidly."

Amy's smile dimmed a little, and she murmured, "Thank you, Mrs Pearce, you're very kind."

Lena sighed, and dropped her head to rest on her mother's shoulder. If Lena had been the sort to fall in love, she'd often thought it would have had to have been with Amy. Not that Amy would ever have chosen her rather than Joe Martin, so no doubt it was just as well that Lena preferred the freedom of being an adventurer.

"That's one and six," Ruth concluded, having noted down Amy's purchases in her ledger and added them up. As she received the coins from Amy, and unlocked the cash drawer to put them away, Ruth chided them. "What is all this formality from you both, when you've known each other since you were a pair of lasses coming home from school with tangled hair and muddied knees!"

Amy blushed a little, and Lena laughed, squeezing her mother's waist hard enough to distract her. "I have a question for you, Amy, if you have a moment."

"Of course, Lena."

Ruth stowed Amy's purchases into her string bag for her, and then turned away to potter along the shelves, adjusting the display to fill the day's gaps.

"Do we have a Needlework Group here? You know, the Red Cross thing, making clothes and stuff for the soldiers."

"We do!" Amy replied, eyes bright with curiosity. "If you mean the Needlework *Guild*. Gillian Wright runs it, and we meet twice a week or so, at her home or mine."

Lena was grinning. "I knew you were the woman to ask."

"I didn't know you knitted, Lena, or sewed."

"I don't, but I have a new member for you."

Amy thought for a moment, and her expression turned shrewd. "Let me guess: Miss Cawkwell of Fields Corner."

Lena just laughed at Amy's perspicacity – or her own transparency.

"She'll be very welcome, Lena. I'll write her a note with the details, and when we're meeting next – I'll bring it in tomorrow, and then *you* can deliver it for me," Amy concluded with a twinkle.

"Thanks, Amy," Lena said, knowing it was useless to try asserting that there were no personal deliveries made to Fields Corner – and anyway, Ruth was listening in, despite making herself busy dusting the shelves, so Lena could hardly risk making her meaning known.

"I'll see you tomorrow, Lena. Goodbye, Mrs Pearce!"

"Goodbye, Amy," they chorused. And with a bright jangle from the bell, Amy left the shop –

which seemed a little darker inside without her smile to light it.

There was an Army truck that wound its way through the village on a regular basis, collecting their excess vegetables and other produce, including Emily's cabbages and Mrs Makepeace's eggs. It had used to come on Monday, Wednesday and Friday afternoons, but it was now appearing on other days, too, with the only exception so far being Sundays – and in the mornings as well as the afternoons. The truck was a rackety old thing, so Lena knew exactly which vehicle was coming up behind her bicycle as she began her rounds early the next day.

The truck caught up with her at a point where the lane narrowed before turning a tight corner, so she quit pedalling and pulled over to the side to let it pass.

The driver gave a brief salute of thanks as he passed, and Lena didn't remount immediately but waited for him to negotiate the turn. So she had an unimpeded view of what was contained in the back of the truck that morning. And it wasn't cabbages.

There were three or four army types sitting on a wooden bench down one side, with Amy's husband Joe Martin perched tensely near the tailgate, apparently lost in his own thoughts. Sitting opposite him was Eva Rowan, sharply dressed in a tweed jacket and matching narrow skirt, with her hair bound up in a tight bun and her make-up as gloriously dramatic as Lena had ever seen it. Eva stared back at her with a stony expression that gave nothing away.

A moment later the truck had turned the corner and was picking up speed as the lane straightened out again.

Lena pushed off and followed slowly, not bothering to try chasing after the truck. She didn't want to breathe the exhaust fumes, and neither did she want to provoke Eva. This must be something to do with the work Eva had mentioned, which had sounded all very clandestine. Lena wondered if Joe Martin was involved in that work as well, or if he had other business to attend to. Amy had said something about him having ongoing physical rehabilitation, so maybe Joe simply had a medical appointment that the army was prepared to transport him to.

It was all very mysterious, but also none of her business! Lena knew well enough that curiosity wasn't exactly welcome during wartime. One more reason to wish that it was all over, and soon, and she could go back to being harmlessly nosy.

As she rode through the lingering fumes, Lena looked forward to the day when they'd be rid of that ugly old truck, as well, and peace – in all senses of the word – would return to the village.

Chapter Three

It wasn't milking day, and there was no answer that afternoon when Lena knocked at the front door of Fields Corner, so she made her way around to the back garden, just in case. Her heart thudded as she rounded the corner to find Miss Cawkwell clearing the overgrown vegetable garden with a cumbersome old gardening fork. Miss Cawkwell had yet to make much progress, but the task appeared dauntingly large so that wasn't such a surprise.

"Good afternoon, Sylvie!" Lena called, not wanting to startle the woman by suddenly appearing at her shoulder.

Miss Cawkwell stopped work, and turned to greet her with a smile – a small smile but so warm that Lena's heart thudded once more. "It's a pleasure to see you, Lena. How are you?"

"I'm well, thank you." She produced a letter, and held it up between two fingers as she drew close. "I have mail for you."

Miss Cawkwell took the letter with thanks, and then paused for a moment, frowning down at the envelope. "No stamp?"

Lena laughed. "No, it's from Amy – Mrs Martin – about the Needlework Group – Guild, I mean. I wasn't going to take her penny, not when she was doing me a favour. Not that she didn't try to insist!"

A sharp glance from Miss Cawkwell might

have questioned the complications of favours received and bestowed between the three of them, but then she turned her attention to unfastening the envelope and reading the message. "Mrs Martin says I'll be very welcome to join them," Sylvie announced a moment later. "They're meeting at Mrs Martin's home on Thursday afternoon, and then at Mrs Wright's the following Tuesday."

"That's great," Lena said with a grin. "You'll like Amy. She's the sweetest girl in all the world."

"I'll be very happy to meet her," Sylvie responded in perfectly proper tones. But she was considering Lena with an intent curiosity.

"She lives in Piebald Lane. It's quite easy to find from here, just a turn off your way to the village. I can draw you a map, if you like, or at least write the directions."

"But you'll be coming with me, won't you? Or do you want to meet me there?" Sylvie nodded. "Of course you do. You don't want to come all the way out here before turning around and going back again."

Lena took a moment to catch up – then blurted, "But I don't go to these things! I don't know how to knit! Or sew. I – I didn't even know when they met, remember!"

"I'd be happy to teach you to knit."

"Oh! Um..." Learning how to knit would involve time spent with Sylvie. Probably rather a lot of time... Lena could hardly deny she was interested. But: "I'm sure I'd be useless. You don't want your efforts to go to waste."

"Nonsense," Sylvie replied briskly. "If you

can milk a goat, you can knit a pair of socks." She paused for a moment's thought. "You can knit a scarf, at least."

It was just too tempting a prospect. "I'll try, then," said Lena. "Until you get fed up with me."

A droll look seemed to indicate that Sylvie didn't think that likely to happen any time soon. And Lena's heart burst into a potent song.

"She wants to teach me how to knit!" Lena announced when she finally tracked down Emily – who, like Sylvie, was making the most of the sunny afternoon by tending her vegetable garden.

Emily cast Lena a wry smile, and tugged out a rogue weed. "You're talking about Miss Cawkwell, I take it."

Lena laughed. She would have to get used to being so obvious. "Who else, indeed?"

"You're letting her domesticate you already!"

"It's not like that," Lena retorted – and then she shivered at a recurring thought. "Just think of all that time I'll have to spend with her... I'm sure I'll be useless at it. The knitting, I mean."

"So, you'll drag it on as long as you possibly can, will you?"

"Why not, with both of us paying such close attention to each other's fingers...?"

Emily laughed at that, even as she shook her head in despair. "You're incorrigible, Lena Pearce."

"And proud of it!" Lena grinned at her friend, and turned to go – "I'd better get back to the shop. Too many distractions today!" – but then she turned again. “Emily. Have you heard anything about Eva Rowan having some kind of job now? Doing work for the army, I think. She’s very cagey about the details.”

Emily’s expression turned guarded. “Best not to enquire too closely, then.”

“She had all her old science books out when I made a delivery the other day.”

No response. Emily shifted to kneel by another garden bed, and began wielding her knife. “Do you and your Mum want some spinach? There’s plenty here.”

“Thanks, that would be great.” No one refused an offer of food these days. Lena considered her friend carefully. “Aren’t you curious, though? About Eva.”

“Not really.” Emily had her head down, binding together a handful of spinach stalks with a ragged bit of string. “Here you are, then. Give my best wishes to your Mum for me!”

“Will do. Thanks again, Emily.” Lena watched as a ladybird walked over the dark green undulations of a spinach leaf, surprisingly fast, and then lifted off to fly away home. It was obviously time for Lena to do the same.

Lena rode her bicycle to Miss Cawkwell’s early on Thursday afternoon and then the two of them set off for Amy’s home on Piebald Lane. Not much was said, but they strode along at a good pace, shoulder to shoulder, as if marching off to face a common foe.

Amy opened her front door and with a

twinkle of her bright blue eyes immediately dispersed the solemn mood. "Welcome, Lena!" she said with a delightful smile. "And you must be Miss Cawkwell," she added, offering her hand to Sylvie. "What a pleasure it is to meet you."

"Thank you, Mrs Martin," said Miss Cawkwell, shaking Amy's hand. "You are very kind to invite a stranger to your home."

"Any friend of Lena's will always be welcome here, of course." Amy's smile quirked, and she bent her head a little closer as if to confide in Miss Cawkwell. "You've obviously made quite an impression on her!"

A pink blotch appeared on each of Miss Cawkwell's cheeks, but she didn't appear overly discomposed. She stuttered for a moment, then managed to say, "The impression – the *good* impression is mutual, I assure you."

"Save me," muttered Lena, almost at risk of blushing herself. She put an end to the niceties by pushing past Amy and into the house. "Learning to knit will be a lark compared to this!"

Amy ushered Miss Cawkwell in as well, and then led them both to her sitting room. A circle of women sat there on the sofas and relocated dining chairs, all of them busy either knitting with dull green wool or hand-sewing pieces of white fabric together. Lena waited in the background while Amy introduced Miss Cawkwell to Mrs Wright, Mrs Makepeace and the rest. The only person Miss Cawkwell already knew was Mrs Doherty, her landlady and owner of Christabel the goat.

Eventually Miss Cawkwell and Lena were

invited to sit in the last two vacant chairs, obviously saved for the purpose by Amy.

"Do you already have a project underway, Miss Cawkwell?" Amy asked.

"No, I don't," Miss Cawkwell replied. "I have needles and the Red Cross Society pattern book, but I'm afraid I don't have any yarn – I mean, none in a suitable colour."

"We can help you there." Amy fetched a basket full of balls of wool, all in shades of grey-green or dull brown, and invited Miss Cawkwell to help herself. Then Amy brought the basket over to Lena.

"Oh, no," Lena said, sitting back and crossing her arms. "Today I'll just be watching."

"Nonsense," Miss Cawkwell said. "I promised I'd teach Lena how to knit, Mrs Martin. I'll get you started on a scarf, Miss Pearce. I'll cast on and do the first few rows for you. You'll find it much easier to pick it up from there."

Lena made an incoherent protest, which was completely overridden by Amy's beaming approval, so Lena settled in to watch Miss Cawkwell work.

In this task, at least, Miss Cawkwell appeared superbly competent. She produced a pair of knitting needles from her bag, and a printed booklet, briefly consulted a pattern – and then she was off! Within moments, the yarn was wrapped back-and-forth around a few inches of one of the needles – not that it was just wound around the needles, for there was some kind of knot involved, though Lena had completely failed to see the logic of it.

"You'd better not watch me for now," Miss Cawkwell said. "Casting on a stitch isn't quite the same as knitting a stitch, so you might find it confusing."

"Fine by me!" Lena said. She turned her gaze on the fair Amy instead, who offered her a warmly encouraging smile. The rest of the women were busy exchanging glances and the occasional muttered remark with each other, while their hands worked on independently, as if they could sew or knit without conscious thought.

As she looked around the room again, Lena realised that Mrs Bernays was staring across at her, though relatively covert with her head apparently bowed over her knitting. Perhaps Mrs Bernays was overdue a personal delivery... Lena winked at her, and the woman's cheeks went pink. Well, that made two of them now hoping that mail addressed to *Mrs Bernays* would arrive within the next few days.

"I'm ready," Miss Cawkwell announced. "Mrs Martin, may I borrow your work for a moment?"

"Of course, Miss Cawkwell," Amy said, immediately handing over a piece of knitting that was a few inches long and had two needles at the top with yarn wrapped around each of them.

"Do you see, Miss Pearce?" Miss Cawkwell said, shifting on her seat so that they could both look closely at Amy's work. "Each of these rows of Vs," she continued, tracing one line across the width of the piece, is one row of knitting. And each row is formed by these loops on the needles. When we knit across the width, we're forming a row by interlocking another length of yarn with the previous row, stitch by stitch."

"Mmm," Lena managed, hoping she sounded at least half convinced.

"And as we add each row, we're forming a fabric of wool, nice and snug and warm." Miss Cawkwell smiled when she saw that Lena remained doubtful. Having handed Amy's work back with a sweet nod of thanks, Miss Cawkwell turned again to Lena. "Never mind all that for now. It will make more sense later, once you're underway. I'll show you how to form the stitches."

"All right," Lena gamely agreed.

Miss Cawkwell picked up her two needles, one of which had a long line – row – of stitches on it. With a quick little flurry, she wrapped the yarn around the fingers of her left hand, and then she held it all between them so that they could both see clearly. "You make a new stitch by pushing the right-hand needle through the old stitch on the left-hand needle – then you pick up the yarn with your right needle – and bring that loop forward through the old stitch."

"Mmm..." Lena vaguely suspected she would grasp the overall process in the not too distant future, but the specific mechanics of it remained a puzzle.

"With the new stitch safely on the right-hand needle, you pull the old stitch off the left-hand needle – and that's our first stitch of the new row! Now we move on to the next stitch."

Miss Cawkwell slowly created the next stitch, describing what she was doing as she did it, and then knitted a third stitch. Lena tried to pay attention to the wool and the needles rather than Miss Cawkwell's long pale fingers. They were almost elegant as she knitted. Far more coordinated than when she was milking Christabel, as Miss Cawkwell herself had promised. Lena wondered what else Miss Cawkwell might be elegant at...

"Do you want to try?" Miss Cawkwell asked – Lena couldn't help but throw her a wry smirk –

– and there were gasps! First one from nearby, and then more rolled around the room.

Lena froze. It was true that a few recipients of her personal deliveries were in attendance, but didn't each individual keep it a secret? Lena was sure the various women were discreet – they were each married, after all! And had her distracted thoughts even been that transparent...?

"What is this?!" Mrs Makepeace demanded.

Lena risked a glance at Amy, who had also frozen in guilty confusion. Mrs Bernays was staring so hard now that the whites of her eyes were showing. Surely Miss Cawkwell was above suspicion, though. She was a Miss, and therefore unapproachable! Or was Emily the only person to know of Lena's rules...? And Emily wasn't there, of course.

"*That* is the German method!" Mrs Makepeace declared in disapproving tones. After a tense moment, she asked slightly more politely, "You are using the German method of knitting, are you not, Miss Cawkwell?"

Miss Cawkwell looked down at her hands, still holding the yarn and needles as she'd been doing. There was no denial here – though Lena noted that Mrs Bernays quietly dropped her knitting into her lap, as if afraid of guilt by association, no matter how unlikely. Mrs Doherty remained silent. "The Continental method," Miss Cawkwell carefully yet firmly replied. "Yes."

All this consternation was about *knitting* styles...? Lena relaxed for her own sake – but Miss Cawkwell was still the subject of a roomful of suspicious stares. "What's the problem?" Lena asked. "Explain it to those of us who aren't initiated."

"There is a *British* method of knitting," Mrs Makepeace ground out. "That would be *far* more appropriate –"

"We are knitting for our brave *British* soldiers, after all!" someone else chipped in.

"Where did you learn to knit like that?" another woman demanded.

Amy had the courage to offer an unconcerned laugh. "As if our dear soldiers would even know the difference."

"What *is* the difference?" Lena asked her.

"There's no difference at all in the finished garment," Amy replied. "It's a matter of which hand you use to hold the yarn as you knit. There's little more to it than that."

Miss Cawkwell took the prompt, and shifted her yarn to weave through the fingers of her right hand rather than the left. "I can use either method, so I'll switch if that makes you happier."

She sounded reasonable rather than resentful, Lena was impressed to note. Though many in the room seemed even more astounded now, and Mrs Makepeace remarked rather faintly, "How very flexible of you..."

For a moment, Miss Cawkwell's lips pressed together into a flat line, as if she were suppressing a retort – but when she spoke, she still sounded entirely unflappable. "Unless she insists, I won't teach Miss Pearce my foreign ways." Miss Cawkwell turned towards Lena, and said, "Let me show you again how to make a stitch. It is slightly different this way, in how you handle the yarn, and I'm guessing the details have already escaped you anyway."

Lena was curious about other matters, though. "Foreign?" she asked quietly – though the whole room's attention remained on them, so there was no being discreet. "You came here from London, didn't you?"

Miss Cawkwell lifted her free hand to her sternum, as she'd done once before. This time, her fingers seemed to take comfort from touching the bead necklace she wore. "I lived almost ten years in London," she answered, "but I was born and bred – and learned knitting – in Yorkshire."

"Why didn't you go back home to Yorkshire, then?" Mrs Makepeace demanded.

Amy gasped. "Mrs Makepeace, please. Miss Cawkwell is a guest in my home, and a good friend of Lena's, and I won't have her quizzed like this."

Though Lena had to wonder whether her friendship would hinder rather than help Miss Cawkwell's credibility here in the village.

"Thank you, Mrs Martin," Miss Cawkwell

replied smoothly, "but it's all right. The war teaches us to be suspicious, and so it probably should."

Mrs Makepeace cleared her throat, and following a nudge from the woman beside her, managed to say, "If I gave offence –"

"I understand," said Miss Cawkwell, as if this had been the fulsome apology she deserved. "To be frank, there was nowhere for me to go to, back in Yorkshire. But then a friend of a friend mentioned that Fields Corner was available to let, and so I was very glad to come here. It has been splendid to make new friends –" she glanced at Lena and at Amy – "and to find the help and support I looked for –" with a grateful look at Mrs Doherty. "I wasn't expecting to be welcomed so generously."

"We're very glad," concluded Amy, "that you have chosen to make your new home here."

And with that, everyone took the hint and got on with their tasks – and Lena tried to apply her mind to learning how to knit.

"Oh, good heavens!" cried Emily. "What were they so concerned about? Do they honestly think she's a German spy, or something?"

Lena laughed, though without much humour. "There was some talk about passing coded messages via knitting patterns."

"But, really. What on earth would anyone spy on out here? There's nothing within thirty miles of us that's of any interest to anyone. Not to mention we're nowhere near the coast... Unless the Germans want to monitor my cabbage production."

"I'm sure there's *someone somewhere* who'd find your cabbages interesting."

Emily chuckled. "Yes – a whole nation of sauerkraut lovers!"

"Good point and fairly made."

But apparently that was all that could be said about cabbages, even by Emily, for she returned to the previous subject. "How does that work, anyway? Coding messages into your knitting?"

Lena collapsed onto the sofa beside her best friend. "I barely managed the basics today, and I'm guessing that would be in the advanced classes." She frowned, trying to remember the little she'd understood. "It's based on Morse code being dots and dashes, while the knitting stitches are nits and – and pearls. Or something."

"Pearls…?"

"I haven't learnt them yet. I've only done the nits. I could have that wrong! … Come to think of it, I guess the 'nit' stitches are spelt with a 'k'. Like knit and knot."

Emily nodded with mock seriousness. "Far more pleasant. And pearls are pleasanter still! I love pearls. Tell me when you get to that part."

"Will do," Lena promised, as she snuggled up against Emily's side and settled in. She'd probably already missed the outgoing mail, but there'd hardly been anything when she'd checked at midday, and Lena had prepared it as much as possible for Ruth to take care of, just in case the knitting group ran late.

They rested there quiet and comfortable, until at last the twilight fell and Lena must ride home before it got too dark to see where she was going.

When Lena arrived at Fields Corner the next morning, she found Miss Cawkwell outside the gate, about to walk Christabel back to Mrs Doherty's. "Morning, Sylvie! Can I join you?"

"Good morning, Miss Pearce. Your company would be very welcome, of course."

Lena hopped off her bicycle, and walked with it alongside Miss Cawkwell and the goat. "Are we back to being formal?" Lena asked in an anxious tone that was only half ironic.

Miss Cawkwell glanced at her, and then lowered her head for a moment as if considering. Eventually she said, "I'm afraid I made a bad impression yesterday, on your friends and neighbours."

"Nonsense! They're the ones who made a bad impression. Sylvie, I couldn't believe how gracious you were, what with all the ridiculous things they were saying."

"Do you think so...?" Miss Cawkwell sighed. "It was kind of Mrs Martin to be so supportive."

"Told you she's the sweetest thing!"

Another glance, skewed as if Miss Cawkwell was feeling wary but just couldn't help herself. "I hope I didn't embarrass her." She left a beat. "Or you."

"Me? Oh, no. I don't embarrass easy. And Amy wouldn't have said anything she didn't mean."

"Thank you," Miss Cawkwell said, though

she sounded rather pensive despite Lena's reassurance. "I'm glad."

"So, shall I come with you to Gillian Wright's next week?"

A moment passed in which Miss Cawkwell wrestled with Christabel, who was more interested in eating weeds than in walking along the road. Then, still with her head down, Miss Cawkwell said, "If you think I would still be welcome."

"Of course you will be! Anyway, if you stay away, they'll think that only goes to prove their stupid theories."

"The thought had occurred to me," Miss Cawkwell admitted.

They had already reached Mrs Doherty's farmhouse. Miss Cawkwell opened the side gate and led Christabel into the yard, before turning to wait – so Lena hastily propped her bicycle against the fence, and followed her in. They processioned down the side of the house, and found Mrs Doherty in the back, hanging out the last of her washing. The hill that rose immediately beyond the Dohertys' back garden was verdant with sweet-smelling long grass.

Greetings were exchanged while Miss Cawkwell ushered Christabel into a small field off to the side, where she was met by her two eager kids. Then Miss Cawkwell returned to stand by Lena. "Mrs Doherty," she said, "I owe you an apology for any embarrassment I caused you yesterday. I can promise you that I am English through and through, but if you'd rather not let me have Christabel any longer, or stay at Fields Corner,

I would understand."

Lena let out an incoherent protest. Being scrupulous in her dealings was one thing, but surely Miss Cawkwell was now taking it too far...

Mrs Doherty considered her for the space of three heartbeats, before saying, "Seemed to me they were making something of nothing. But that's how these things start, isn't it?"

Which was a rather ambiguous remark. Lena opened her mouth, wanting to know *'What things?'*

But Mrs Doherty was grimacing, and she indicated Lena with a tilt of her chin. "To be plain, Miss Cawkwell, I'm more worried about you keeping company with this rascal."

Lena huffed, and planted her fists on her hips. She might still be suffering from a lack of words, but she would sure as hell fight Mrs Doherty's assertion if she had to.

Miss Cawkwell, however, was amused. "I understand, Mrs Doherty, but while my knitting methods are negotiable, my friendship with Miss Pearce is not."

"Well, then." Mrs Doherty picked up her empty washing basket and propped it on her hip. "I'll see you tomorrow evening when you collect Christabel, Miss Cawkwell!" she called as she turned away and headed towards the house.

"Thank you, Mrs Doherty!" Miss Cawkwell responded. And she turned to usher Lena back out to the road, as if they should depart quickly while the winds were favourable.

The two of them trotted down the path, and spilled out through the gate giggling as if they were girls who'd just escaped school for the day. "Come on, I'll give you a ride," Lena said, mounting the bicycle but standing forward, leaving room for Miss Cawkwell to take the seat.

Miss Cawkwell hesitated, though. "Oh... thank you, but I shouldn't think that's a good idea."

"I know what I'm doing. I've been giving my friends rides since I was a girl."

A bright glance from Miss Cawkwell, almost as if she understood that as innuendo – honestly unintended by Lena, but a perfectly reasonable assumption for anyone who knew her well. Miss Cawkwell's gaze dropped again to the road surface, and she explained, "I was thinking of me, not you. I don't doubt your skills, but I know how awkward I can be. I'm sure I'd have us head over heels – and wheels – before we were halfway home."

Lena laughed, and confessed, "I love a challenge! Hop onto the seat, grab my hips or my waist, and relax into it. Trust me, and I'm sure we'll be fine."

Miss Cawkwell seemed very tempted, as she shifted her weight a little closer even if she didn't quite take a step. Her hands flexed, almost as if she were imagining shaping them to Lena's body.

"Come on, Sylvie," Lena murmured encouragingly...

Another bright flash of her eyes in response to her given name, and then Miss Cawkwell was hitching up her graceless dress a little, and climbing onto the bicycle seat. Lena held the bicycle steady until Miss Cawkwell was settled, with her hands firm on Lena's hips. Which was oh so very nice...

"All right?" Lena asked.

"Yes," Miss Cawkwell replied, sounding a little breathless.

Lena lifted her left foot to the pedal – "Then we're off!" – and leaned forward to get them started. At first they were all slightly wobbly, but within three strokes of the pedals they were travelling smoothly. Lena pushed into it to build up speed, despite Miss Cawkwell's hard grip, and was soon rewarded with a happy laugh and a "*wooo*" from her passenger. Lena laughed, too, and allowed herself to enjoy rocking her hips to and fro while the other woman clung on.

Too soon they were pulling up before the gate at Fields Corner, and Lena was carefully planting her feet on the road's surface to ensure they wouldn't topple over. Miss Cawkwell chuckled again, throatily, and slowly climbed down off the seat, maintaining her hold on Lena until she'd swung her leg back over the bicycle and was standing upright. Even then her hands seemed to linger a moment or two longer than they needed to, and she was standing so close...

Lena turned her head to look at Miss Cawkwell, who was almost pretty with her fine hair windblown and her expression full of fun. Who cared if she was a plain Miss, when she seemed so enticing, and there was always that long elegant neck to admire, if only Lena weren't so snared by Miss Cawkwell's delighted smile.

And was it possible that Miss Cawkwell was feeling enticed, too, when Lena could have sworn she was innocent to the point of naivety...? Lena tested this by easing a bit closer towards Miss Cawkwell – who was, after all, still standing there for no apparent reason – and Lena had her answer a moment later when Miss Cawkwell closed the remaining distance, took the larger bolder leap, and pressed her lips hard to Lena's.

A still moment passed. As a kiss, it lacked finesse, and was fervent enough to be almost painful, but Lena's heart thudded powerfully in response.

Then Miss Cawkwell drew back and took a step away. She seemed more colourful than she had before, as if the kiss or maybe just the bicycle ride had sparked new life through her, and the neutral tones were fleeing from its path.

"Sylvie," Lena said – or rather whispered, for she seemed to have had the breath knocked out of her. How could she explain that this just wasn't what Lena was looking for? There was no place for a plain Miss in the life that Lena had built for herself.

Miss Cawkwell was still smiling, though in a quieter kind of way now. "You need to get back to the shop, I suppose?"

"Yes," said Lena.

"Perhaps I'll see you tomorrow?" Her tone and expression indicated that Miss Cawkwell hoped this would be so.

"Yes," Lena agreed, if only because she was grateful for being dismissed so readily today. Honestly, she had thought Miss Cawkwell far too unworldly to be in any danger of misunderstandings...

"Good afternoon, then, Lena!"

Miss Cawkwell took another step back towards the gate, and Lena managed to stir herself enough to place a foot on the pedals and push off. "Goodbye!" she called back as she gathered pace. And perhaps there was a happy "Goodbye!" called after her, or perhaps Lena imagined it as the wind whisked past her ears.

Chapter Four

Lena was replenishing the high shelves of tea and cocoa early that evening, when a grinding growl announced the Army truck approaching from the direction of town. It usually drove through the village without stopping, so Lena paid it no mind – until a stutter of gears and squeal of brakes announced that today was different. With a great deal of loud drama, the truck pulled up directly outside the shop, casting a long shadow up the windows in the westering sun.

Someone was being helped down from the back of the truck while it idled. Lena sighed, and climbed down the ladder to the floor. She didn't need to see the silhouette or hear the murmured conversation to know who it would be. A moment later the front door opened, and the tinkle of the bell was drowned out by the truck lurching back into motion. The door swung closed, the noise of the truck faded away – and Eva Rowan said, "Good evening, Lena."

"How can I help you, Mrs Rowan?" Lena took up a position by the cash drawer.

"A small loaf of bread and four eggs, thank you, Miss Pearce," Eva replied as she stalked towards Lena. Those shapely legs in her high heels, topped by her swaying hips, were mesmerising.

Lena instead turned her attention to carefully placing the eggs in a paper bag with a handful of straw to protect them. She returned to the counter with the bag of eggs and the loaf, and began writing up the sale in the ledger.

Eva stood close to the high counter, and whispered, "Why haven't you visited me?"

"I delivered your mail," Lena said, somewhat quieter than usual.

"I told you I'd be at work during the day! You'll have to come in the evenings."

"Hush..." Lena glanced behind her at the door through to the back rooms, which stood open. "Mum's here," she whispered to Eva. "Somewhere. Maybe she's upstairs."

Eva pushed closer, as far as she was able, and hissed, "The truck will be back any moment. They're taking Joe Martin home, and then coming back for me. Come *on*, Lena!"

"I told you it doesn't work like that," she insisted. "That's sixpence," Lena added in her normal tones, if somewhat strained.

"You won't come in the evenings?"

"No."

"Then come for Sunday dinner after church."

"No!"

Eva stood upright again, and searched in her purse for coins. A faint grumble announced the imminent return of the truck. Eva dropped the sixpence on the countertop rather than place it in Lena's hand. "I don't know why you're denying yourself," Eva said sharply, gathering up her purchases. "I do an *excellent* roast, on rations or not!"

Lena couldn't help herself: the corners of her mouth twitched in amusement at the double meaning. But still she shook her head, and stood back. She'd said her piece, and wasn't going to change her mind.

Eva nodded a curt farewell, and strode out of the shop, letting the door swing closed behind her.

And Lena almost blurted out loud, *'It's not because Miss Cawkwell kissed me!'*

Because it wasn't.

"Are you actually left-handed?" Miss Cawkwell whispered to Lena under cover of the Needlework Guild's hubbub of discussion.

Lena snorted as quietly as she could. She'd been so proud of completing another row of her scarf without guidance, but it seemed she'd mangled it. "No...?"

Miss Cawkwell wasn't convinced. "Try it this way around," and she switched her own knitting so the needles and the yarn were all in the opposite hands, demonstrating her technique with a few stitches.

Lena tried to do the same, but felt clumsier than ever. Still, she persisted, just in case – until the hubbub caught her attention by turning indignant.

"Knots do not belong in knitted garments!" Mrs Makepeace was declaring loudly.

"I'm not saying they do," countered the handsome Gillian Wright, "in ordinary circumstances."

"In *any* circumstances."

"I had just heard that knotting the yarn at various lengths is another way of passing coded messages. I suppose you could only read it once the garment was unravelled, but I –"

"Unravelled!" Mrs Makepeace seemed horrified. She looked around the room to enlist support – and her gaze snagged on something even more alarming. "What are you doing *now*, Miss Cawkwell?" she demanded.

Miss Cawkwell let her hands fall to her lap, but her posture remained upright. "I was knitting left-handed, Mrs Makepeace."

"You are flexible, indeed!"

"A temporary measure," Miss Cawkwell continued, "though I see no harm in it."

Lena protested, "What's wrong with being ambi– ambivalent?"

"*Not* ambilevous," Mrs Wright countered with an irrepressible giggle.

"Ambidextrous," Amy provided. "And there's no harm in it at all."

Mrs Makepeace was silenced, at least for the moment. Miss Cawkwell turned towards Lena, switched her own knitting back, and with a nod indicated that Lena should do the same. Lena only complied because knitting left-handed had seemed even more impossible.

A few quietly industrious minutes passed, before Amy spoke up again. "My Joe – my husband," she added, turning to Miss Cawkwell. "He came home to us recently. Joe has been advised to take up a craft as part of his rehabilitation. And of course he wants to contribute to the war effort. So I hope none of you will mind if Joe joins us – at least when we meet at our home on Thursdays."

"Hurrah!" Lena cried out. "Another beginner!"

"Mr Martin will be welcome here on Tuesdays as well, if you like," Mrs Wright said firmly.

There was a general murmuring of agreement, though Lena noticed a few doubtful glances exchanged. His presence would probably curtail certain topics of conversation, but it wasn't as if the women didn't have a hundred opportunities a week to talk in confidence, what with almost all the men gone from the village.

Amy was smiling in gratitude. "I'm not sure about Tuesdays, Gillian. He has medical appointments, and they have him doing part-time work, as well. But I will ask him."

"It will be nice to have a man around," Mrs Bernays said, with a blush for that man's wife and a self-conscious glance at Lena.

"I'll be glad to meet him," said Miss Cawkwell.

"Though knowing Joe," Lena reflected, "my scarf will still look shabby by comparison."

"You are all so very kind," Amy concluded. Though to be honest, Lena thought, who could refuse the delectable Amy anything at all?

Lena's mail delivery route had been established by her Uncle Bill before she was even born, and had needed few adjustments over the years. The village had grown very slowly, with few dwellings being built or restored either there or in the surrounding farmlands. So, when a small package at last arrived for Mrs Bernays, Lena knew exactly when she'd be making the delivery that morning: early enough that the air would still be chilled, that Mrs Bernays would still be warmly enfolded in her dressing gown with her hair pinned in curls, that she would still be half asleep with her tea half drunk.

Which all made for a sweet encounter, with this short, soft woman lifting her face to Lena's to offer a kiss and receive one in turn. It was all they ever did together, and it was truly lovely.

As Lena had feared, Joe Martin's knitting was neat and precise, and his scarf was already three times the length of hers. "You can't tell me you're only just learning this now!" she protested.

Joe didn't smile, as he might once have done, but he wrinkled his nose at Lena, and said, "I have a wonderful teacher." At which Amy's cheeks coloured with pleasure.

"So do I!" Lena responded. "I guess *my* teacher is cursed with a poor student."

"You're doing very well," Miss Cawkwell declared stoutly, "for someone who gave no thought to knitting until a week ago."

"You're both excellent students," Amy chimed in.

Lena became conscious that the rest of the room had gone quiet, and their heads were bent over their knitting as their hands continued an industrious rhythm. She glanced at Sylvie to her right, who was putting on a show of obliviousness –

and Amy and Joe on her left, who also had their heads down though they were curved towards each other as if for mutual support. The quiet clickety-clack of knitting needles was supplemented by a faint but more jittery beat.

"The weather has been particularly kind these past couple of weeks," Gillian Wright observed to the room at large. "My vegetable garden is having a superb growing season. I trust everyone is enjoying the same."

"Yes," Miss Cawkwell answered when it seemed that no one else would do more than nod in agreement. "I can hardly keep up with the garden beds at Fields Corner –"

"It's fair to say they had a head start!" said Lena.

"This is a beautiful part of the country," Miss Cawkwell concluded. "So verdant!"

"Thank you, yes," said Gillian. "We are blessed to live here."

And then the silence returned. Lena wondered why no one questioned the fields of grass running amok in the kind weather.

Gillian Wright tried a different topic, though lowering her voice to be slightly more confidential. "Mrs Makepeace, how are Eddie and Edie faring?"

"Good weather or not, their asthma's no better," was the reply, weighted with worry.

"Eddie and Edie?" Miss Cawkwell asked in a whisper.

"Mrs Makepeace's grandchildren," Amy quietly supplied.

"*Twins*," Lena added, trying not to get

caught rolling her eyes at the poor kids' given names. Either name on its own would be fine, but together they were no doubt doomed to be teased and quizzed all their lives.

Silence again. Maybe Lena had failed in her attempt at tact. More than likely, she reflected. In any case, everyone was studiously ignoring *something*, and...

And Lena belatedly realised that it was Joe's foot tapping as his left knee shook and trembled that everyone was ignoring. It seemed to be a nervous tic – and the more anxious he became, the more pronounced the tic.

Well, it wasn't as if everyone's attention wasn't already focussed entirely on Joe despite Mrs Wright's attempted diversions. Lena began tapping her foot, too, introducing a more regular beat. And then she burst into song. "*It's a long way to Tipperary, it's a long way to go.*"

Thankfully everyone joined in: "*It's a long way to Tipperary, to the sweetest girl I know.*"

Lena couldn't help but glance at Amy on those last words – and her attention was caught by Joe, whose legs were almost at rest again, but who was doubled up laughing with his face in his hands. When he saw her looking, he said confidentially, "We don't actually sing that Over There. At least, not *those* words."

"No? What do you sing?"

Joe grinned, and tipped his head towards the roomful of women. "Nothing I can repeat here!"

The Needlework Guild belted out five oddly raucous choruses of *Tipperary*, and then Gillian led them into a stirring rendition of *Till the Boys Come Home.* Joe sat there concentrating hard on his knitting, more amused – wryly amused – than moved.

Lena was surprised to see that it was Miss Cawkwell who was most affected. She was quiet, and it seemed she had tears in her eyes. When she finally noticed that Lena was watching her with concern, Miss Cawkwell turned towards them and said to Joe, "I'm so sorry for all you've endured, Mr Martin."

Joe sat up straighter again, and nodded in solemn acknowledgement. "Thank you, Miss Cawkwell."

"Sylvie," Lena murmured, reaching to grasp Miss Cawkwell's nearest hand in hers for a moment. The two of them shared a wobbly smile. And then, while Gillian continued to hold the focus of the rest of the group, Amy, Joe and Sylvie got on with their knitting – and Lena persisted with her best efforts.

"Good," Eva Rowan said brusquely as she swung open her front door.

Lena froze on the doormat, holding the mail she'd been about to slip through the letter box. "You're here!" she exclaimed.

"Yes. Come in." Eva was standing back with the door wide open, but when Lena still hesitated, she added, "Don't worry, I won't drag you down to the bedroom." An eyebrow arched sharply. "Unless you want to be dragged."

Lena finally stepped in and placed the letters

on the hallstand. Eva was as perfectly made-up, coiffed, and dressed as she ever was. "Not working today?" Lena asked, leading the way into the dining room, where even more books and notepads were strewn across the table along with files and folders.

"I'm writing up a report. There are fewer distractions here."

"And yet..." *you invited me in.*

Eva smirked at her as if certain distractions were still welcome. However, she said, "I was curious about this Miss Cawkwell of yours."

"Of mine?"

"Joe mentioned her as your particular friend."

"Joe Martin?" Lena shook her head in disbelief. Eva and Joe seemed an unlikely pair of gossips! Lena was surprised they even talked to each other. "What does any of this have to do with anything?"

"The country is at war, Lena," Eva replied flatly. "It's not unexpected that we're curious about newcomers."

Lena stubbornly remained silent for long moments, but eventually figured it was best to deal with unwarranted speculations sooner rather than later. "Miss Cawkwell moved down from London. A friend of hers knew that Mrs Doherty wanted to rent out Fields Corner. There's nothing more to it than that."

"Are you *sure*?"

"Who would *want* to live in London with all this going on? I don't know why you're all so keen to read anything more into Sylvie wanting to move

– Miss Cawkwell, I mean. And to a place where she already had one friend, at least."

"So, you're assuming the best."

"That's what we've always done around here – isn't it? Does a war mean we have to start assuming the worst?"

Eva considered her through narrowed eyes. "Not necessarily. But 'a friend of a friend' is conveniently vague. It might mean nothing at all."

Lena huffed in impatience and turned to leave. "I've got letters to deliver."

"Have fun!" Eva called with a false brightness as Lena collected her bicycle.

Lena responded with a glower. As she rode off, however, Lena found herself wondering if it were possible that she'd been completely taken in. Miss Cawkwell didn't seem to have a sinister bone in her body... Mrs Doherty had deemed her acceptable as a tenant... Amy and Gillian had welcomed Sylvie – but was that for Lena's sake alone...?

By the time she was home again, Lena had shaken off the doubts again – except for one. She really had to wonder if she was as perceptive as she liked to think herself.

Chapter Five

The nearest Telegraph Office was in town, so Lena was rarely involved in directly delivering telegrams. However, whenever a telegram messenger came to the village, they usually did the courtesy of stopping by to alert Lena or her mother. Especially when the telegram came from the War Office.

When the familiar Morgan Runabout pulled up outside the shop, Lena strode out there. She didn't recognise the messenger driving it.

"Miss Pearce?"

"Yes."

There was no further introduction or chat; the messenger simply held out the telegram in its envelope so that Lena could read the address. *Mrs Doherty...*

"Next left, and second right," Lena said. "Then half a mile, and it's a farmhouse on your right."

The messenger nodded her thanks, released the handbrake, and drove away.

Lena dashed back inside. "War Office," she tersely informed Ruth. "Mrs Doherty."

"You'll fetch Gillian?"

"On my way," Lena replied, wheeling her bicycle out the back door.

"Take care!" Ruth called after her.

Lena lifted a hand in acknowledgement – and then she was off, flying along the familiar lanes as fast as her legs could drive her, heart thumping with purpose.

Mrs Wright immediately knew why Lena was there, of course – "Telegram?" – and was collecting her gloves and handbag from the hallstand even while Lena was replying – "Mrs Doherty" – and closing the front door behind her. Lena was still breathing hard from her exertions.

"I'll see you there?" Mrs Wright asked, pausing beside Lena where she stood on the path.

Lena nodded. Of course. Months into the war, and this was already too horribly familiar. Mrs Wright would drive to the recipient of bad news to offer comfort and support, and Lena would follow on her bicycle, ready to help if errands needed running or messages needed delivering.

If there were family members or friends to alert, Lena would do that, too. This time, she said, "I'll tell Miss Cawkwell on the way."

Mrs Wright looked at her for a moment, as if she could see the spike in Lena's heartbeat when that name was spoken. And then Gillian Wright stepped closer, slid a hand around Lena's nape, and pressed a kiss to her forehead. The spike stuttered and then doubled for a moment.

"Of course," Mrs Wright said – and she smiled that wide, beautiful smile of hers, the one she'd been blessing people with for so long that the years had etched it into her fine skin. "Of course. I'll see you there."

Miss Cawkwell was on her knees weeding the front garden at Fields Corner when Lena arrived.

"Welcome, Lena!" she cried, rising to her feet in an endearingly ungainly fashion, and then walking towards the gate. "Do you have mail for me today?"

"No..." Lena let herself in through the gate, and then stood before Miss Cawkwell, considering for a moment. "Sylvie... I'm not sure how well you know Mrs Doherty and her family. I'm not sure how close you are."

"Oh!" Miss Cawkwell turned thoughtful but didn't seem overly concerned. "Well –"

Lena blundered on. "She received a telegram, you see. From the War Office. Which... might not be the *worst* news – but it's never good."

"Ah. And you wondered if I'd be of use to her?"

Lena nodded.

"I'm her neighbour and her tenant, at least. I'll help if I can."

"I'll come with you," Lena said. She waited while Miss Cawkwell went inside to wash her hands and take off her apron, and then the two of them began walking down the road, with Lena wheeling her bicycle. "I could give you a ride?" she offered.

"Is it *very* urgent, do you think?"

"Mrs Wright is on her way – probably already there."

"It would only save us a few minutes, and I would instead like to explain..."

Lena made an encouraging sound, and kept walking at the same steady pace, her gaze on the road ahead to avoid making Sylvie feel any more self-conscious than she already did.

Soon enough, Miss Cawkwell began, "I had a... particular friend in London. We are no longer... We disagreed on so much! *So* much."

A pause threatened to lengthen, so Lena and her curiosity prompted, "You're no longer together?"

"Nor even friends," Miss Cawkwell confirmed with a sigh – though she seemed no more than a little sad about it. "But Miss Perry helped when I wanted to move away. Mrs Doherty is her cousin, so she wrote to her about Fields Corner."

They walked on in silence. Miss Cawkwell seemed to have reached the end of her tale. As they turned the last bend and glimpsed the farmhouse, Lena couldn't resist. She slowed, and looked at Sylvie, and said, "Miss Perry was your... *particular* friend...?"

Sylvie nodded, just once, shakily. Lena reached a hand to grasp Sylvie's, which grasped hers in turn.

"Then, let's go see how we can help her cousin," Lena concluded.

Sylvie smiled, still shaky but also glad and grateful. "Yes, let's." They continued holding hands until they arrived at Mrs Doherty's and were forced to deal with the bicycle and the gate.

In the end, Lena and Miss Cawkwell weren't needed for long. Mrs Makepeace had already been visiting when the telegram was delivered, and Gillian Wright could always manage anything and everything. Miss Cawkwell made and served a fresh pot of tea, but once this was drunk, she and Lena were shooed away.

"Don't forget to take Christabel with you!" Mrs Doherty called out at the last moment.

Mr Doherty was missing in action. Lena had felt a clutch of fear in her gut when Gillian told them, but Mrs Doherty seemed little more than nervous, for now at least. "I woke up this morning," she announced, her voice shaking only slightly, "knowing that he would come home to me. Like Joe Martin came home. Maybe he'll get hurt. A man can hardly go to war without getting hurt in some way or other. But Fred will come home. I know it."

"I'm looking forward to meeting him," Miss Cawkwell had responded in calm but firm tones. "I'll be so very glad to welcome him home."

Now, as Miss Cawkwell walked beside her through the quiet country lanes – leading the goat while Lena wheeled her bicycle – Lena asked, "Do you believe her? That she knows he'll come home?"

Miss Cawkwell looked at her for a moment, as if considering how best to answer.

"I don't!" Lena blurted, giving her permission to be sceptical.

"I don't either, really," Sylvie agreed. "But part of me envies... being *able* to believe – no, perhaps *wanting* to believe so strongly in one's partner."

"You and Miss Perry...?"

Sylvie laughed under her breath, a gentle wry scoffing kind of laugh. "I can't deny I cared very much for her – as I believe she did for me. But we never had that kind of faith in each other."

"Faith?" Lena responded. "I mean..." What *did* she mean? Lena wrinkled her brow in the hopes that would help her think. "I mean, isn't faith about knowing rather than believing? Or... no, the other way round."

"Believing without evidence or proof," Miss Cawkwell supplied. "Believing so deeply that it feels like knowledge."

"And you want to –"

"If it's even possible –" Miss Cawkwell took a breath, and smiled somewhat awkwardly. "Well, to put all one's faith in one's partner... Perhaps that's too much to expect in this world."

And they were silent for the few minutes it took them to reach the front gate of Fields Corner. Miss Cawkwell ushered Christabel into the garden, and then paused as if unsure whether to invite Lena in or say farewell.

"Do you want help with the weeding?" Lena asked.

"Christabel's taking care of that!" And it was true that the goat was already munching away at the yellow-flowered plants she favoured. After a moment, Sylvie suggested, "Perhaps we could continue with our knitting? If your duties aren't calling you away. I fixed your scarf."

"My duties can wait," Lena replied, guiltily enjoying a slight sense of mischief.

"Then do please join me," Sylvie said, with a clumsy welcoming sweep of her arm.

It would take a far better person than Lena Pearce to resist.

They sat outside in the sunshine, Miss Cawkwell insisting that Lena take the milking stool, and herself sitting on an old wooden crate. Lena took a moment to examine the scarf she was knitting, but couldn't even see where the hole had been. "How did you do that? You didn't just start the whole thing over, did you?"

Miss Cawkwell laughed. "No, you'd dropped a stitch, and I picked it back up again. Once you're feeling more confident, I'll show you how."

"Definitely not ready for that yet," Lena muttered.

"You will be soon, though. All you need is an idea of how the stitches act together to form the fabric. Then it's easy enough to fix a problem like that."

Lena remained sceptical, but bent her head over the needles and diligently made some progress. Two uneven rows later, she straightened up, ready for a break.

Miss Cawkwell's hands were still busily working away as if they were independent creatures with no need of her awareness let alone control. However, seeing that Lena was no longer concentrating, Miss Cawkwell laid her hands in her lap, and offered a slight smile. After a moment, she began, "I don't want to pry..."

"About me? Go ahead!"

"Thank you," she responded in a warm tone.

"But no... About Mrs Doherty."

"Go on, then." Lena frowned a little. "I trust you."

"You trust me not to ask – or expect you to tell – anything inappropriate?"

"Exactly." Lena was beginning to realise how very much cleverer Miss Cawkwell was than Lena herself. But that was all right. Lena still trusted her. There was a solid core of good in there, untouched by the physical clumsiness and occasional social ineptness. Lena found that she was sure of it.

"So... Mr Doherty went to war," Miss Cawkwell began slowly, "and Mrs Doherty is left to work the farm..."

"Yes."

"But they hold a lot of land that doesn't seem to be used. A *lot* of land..."

Lena nodded, all too aware of the empty fields with the grass growing long. It was beautiful, and a bit wild, but not how things were supposed to be. "She kept the goats and the chickens," Lena said.

"For her own use," Miss Cawkwell agreed. "And for her neighbours," she added with a nod towards Christabel. "But from what I've seen, she farms maybe an acre or two of land, just as any country household might do. The greater part of their land –"

"– has been left empty, yes." Lena took a breath. "They used to graze sheep, before the war."

Miss Cawkwell picked up that there was more to the story. "What happened to the sheep?"

"I don't know! No one seems to know – and no one wants to talk about it."

This had the desired effect of intriguing Miss Cawkwell.

"It wasn't just the Dohertys' flock, either; it was everyone's around here. The army took them for 'safekeeping'. And it was very sudden. They were all gone within a day or two."

"The army wanted the meat, I suppose, to supply the troops."

"But there's no reason why the sheep couldn't stay here and graze their home pastures in the meantime. It's not as if we couldn't continue shepherding with the men gone."

Miss Cawkwell was puzzling over this. "And they said 'safekeeping'? Implying that they would be maintaining the flocks rather than immediately slaughtering them?"

"Exactly." Lena shook her head. It wasn't as if they were likely to ever know the answers, but at least now someone else agreed that there were questions to be asked. "Something strange is going on."

"It's not that...? Well, we're quite isolated here. Did they want to hold them in a more convenient location?"

"And let all this good pasture go to waste? Doesn't make much sense, not to me anyway. And there is an army base nearby. Have you seen the truck that comes through here, almost every day now? Or *heard* it, more likely, horrible noisy thing that it is. They collect our spare vegetables and such. So we're not *that* inconvenient."

Miss Cawkwell was looking at her very directly. "Where's the base?"

Lena took a breath, and winced on the inside. "Why do you want to know?"

And Miss Cawkwell immediately withdrew. Picking up her knitting again, she said crisply, "I apologise, Miss Pearce. I was just curious. This county is unfamiliar to me, and I hadn't realised there was any such thing nearby."

"No, *I'm* sorry. I *do* trust you. But it's meant to be a secret, do you see?" Lena got up and went to sit cross-legged on the grass at Miss Cawkwell's feet. "Best I can tell is that they're using an old factory a few miles north of here. It even had its own little airfield – not that anything ever flies over the village, or not that I've noticed. Anyway, we're not meant to know about the factory being used again... but a couple of people from the village work there, I think, so I guess they're just relying on everyone keeping quiet."

Miss Cawkwell nodded. "Then I shall let you do so and quit troubling you with my questions."

"It's no trouble. I have questions, too." However, Lena got up again, returned to the milking stool, and picked up her knitting.

When they spoke again, it was of innocuous matters.

A couple of days later, one of the town's taxis pulled up outside the shop, and the driver got out. Lena went to meet her. Another new face, another request for directions to Mrs Doherty's. Lena obliged, and then couldn't resist looking at the taxi's passenger before they drove off again.

A woman maybe around her own age, with an attractive profile, and honey-coloured hair worn up in a tidy bun. Attired in a prim white frock and white gloves, sitting perfectly upright. Looking straight ahead and paying no attention to Lena being nosy. Everything about this woman was neat and pretty and London-ish.

Not even a glance from her, despite a wave from the driver as the taxi pulled away.

Lena felt a clutch of dread as she realised who this must be. Miss Cawkwell's former girlfriend – or maybe not so former.

Miss Perry.

Chapter Six

"Very pretty," said Lena. "Very neat." *Everything that I am not.*

"Yes, that does sound like her," Miss Cawkwell agreed. She seemed nervous: her gaze was flickering from one place to another, and her hands trembled. But then she fixed on Lena with a pleading look – and Lena had to wonder if Miss Cawkwell was thinking exactly the same thing. *Everything that I am not.*

A moment later, Miss Cawkwell had regained enough equanimity to say, "I was about to walk Christabel back home. I had better take the opportunity to welcome her. Would you –? That is, if you have the time, would you care to come with me and meet her?"

"Sure," said Lena, though she didn't feel entirely certain. But curiosity won out, and maybe even the slightest hint of... possessiveness. Lena frowned. That was unexpected.

"We needn't stay long, but it would be impolite to..."

"Of course," she affirmed. It had already been an hour or more since Miss Perry arrived, as Lena had had to finish restocking the shop's shelves as she'd promised Ruth she'd do. "Let's go now, if you're ready."

Miss Cawkwell nodded, and picked up a baggy hat because it was a sunny day – cast the hat a doubtful glance – and ushered Lena back towards the front door.

But before they left, Lena took Miss Cawkwell's hand in hers, and lifted it to her lips for a kiss. She was rewarded for the gesture with a wobbly smile.

Introductions were made in Mrs Doherty's kitchen, where a pot of tea was brewing. "How do you do, Miss Pearce?" said Miss Perry, offering her right hand *sans* glove.

"How d'you do," Lena mumbled in reply, shaking hands before joining the others in sitting at the table. She had never felt so self-conscious in her *life*. It required an effort not to reach up and feel how many pins were still fixed in her hair. She reckoned she lost at least one or two each day – she'd run out of them before the year was out at this rate, and no doubt hairpins were in short supply due to the war already or would be soon...

Lena dragged her attention back to present concerns, and watched Sylvie as she exchanged the safer sort of news with Miss Perry. Despite her polite and occasionally stilted tones, Sylvie seemed comfortable enough in a physical way, as if she and Miss Perry had been familiar for a long time. Perhaps a very long time. And Miss Perry seemed comfortable, too. She sat upright, with perfect posture, but was somehow also relaxed, as if propriety was her natural state.

For a moment as they recalled some shared memory, Miss Perry's smile in Sylvie's direction grew affectionate and was returned in kind. Lena glanced at Mrs Doherty, wondering if she knew that these two had been girlfriends... Maybe not.

Mrs Doherty was – well, she looked pale and careworn, as anyone would whose husband had been declared missing in action. (Which Lena had to assume meant it was probable he'd been killed. It was just that the army wasn't sure yet. Was everyone in the village thinking the same? Probably – though no one had said it out loud.) So, Mrs Doherty was obviously wrung out with worry but otherwise she seemed grateful for her cousin's visit and even a little pleased for her tenant to be reunited with her friend.

"A week at least," Miss Perry was saying in response to Miss Cawkwell's query about how long she was staying. "More, if I can be of use."

Lena couldn't help but look at Miss Perry's delicate white dress and wonder how long it would remain pristine if their visitor intended mucking in with the goats.

"Don't worry, Miss Pearce. I brought my working clothes as well." Miss Perry was smiling at her in mild amusement.

"Oh! Sorry, I was just thinking 'what a beautiful dress', Miss Perry, and –"

"No need to apologise. And please – call me Win." Such a charming smile, too...

"Thank you, Win," she acknowledged. "I'm Lena."

A pleased nod, and then Miss Perry returned her attention to Miss Cawkwell. "I've brought some of your books, Sylvie. Shall I fetch them for you? If it's not convenient now, I can bring them to you on another day."

"That was very thoughtful of you, Win! Now would be wonderful. Especially if Lena doesn't mind me using the basket on her bicycle."

Lena didn't mind at all.

Soon a small pile of books bundled together with string was placed on the table near Sylvie. Lena tilted her head a little to read the titles on the spines: *The Convert*; *Middlemarch*; *No Surrender*; *Plays Unpleasant*; *Prisons & Prisoners*; *The Story of an African Farm*. Lena hadn't heard of any of them, but they obviously meant a great deal to Sylvie, who was trying to suppress a happy smile in this grieving household.

"Shall I send you more once I'm back in London?" Win asked. "Or all of them...?"

Underlying this was Win's real question, Lena surmised: *'How much longer are you staying here, Sylvie?'*

"I'd appreciate having them all here, thank you, Win. But please don't go out of your way. Once my plans are more settled, I can come up to London to sort things out, one way or the other."

"I understand," said Win in a grave tone.

At which point, Mrs Doherty happened to rise to take the empty teapot to the sink – and Miss Cawkwell stood promptly, too – so Lena followed suit. It seemed that Sylvie was ready for the visit to be over.

They said their farewells, and then it was just the two of them walking slowly down the quiet lane, with Sylvie holding the books in both arms, hugging them to her rather than giving them over to the bicycle basket. She seemed to be thinking, but not so deeply that Lena felt she couldn't interrupt. She wasn't hurrying, either, as if needing to reach the safety of home. Not that Lena had anything particularly intelligent to say. But she was curious. Very curious.

After about five minutes of silent companionship, Lena declared, "Well, *she's* pretty amazing, isn't she!"

"Win?" Sylvie smiled a little. "Which isn't short for 'Winifred', by the way, but 'Winsome'."

Lena groaned appreciatively. "She's *perfect*."

Sylvie shifted the books into the crook of one arm and reached to hold Lena's hand. They continued on for a few paces – before Sylvie said, with her gaze averted, "You're probably wondering what she saw in me."

"Not at all." Lena jiggled her hand until Sylvie looked at her again. "Not wondering. I know what *I* see in you – and she knows you better than I do, so she'd have all the more to see."

"You're very kind, Lena."

Which prompted a laugh. "You're probably the only person in this village who'd say so."

Sylvie just cast her a wry look as if she didn't believe her. Which was a worry. Because, really, when a woman was used to the perfections of the neat, pretty Winsome Perry, what could she possibly find of interest in scrappy, tomboyish Lena Pearce? Especially if their friendship had been built so far on generous impressions that would eventually prove to be false.

But then maybe Sylvie Cawkwell – who until

today had seemed so confident in her own skin, in her own mind – maybe she also felt inadequate when compared to Win. It wasn't difficult to imagine Sylvie wanting to *die* of awkwardness at Win's side.

On which thought, the two of them drifted to a halt, and Lena found that they were at Miss Cawkwell's front gate.

They stood there for a moment, their hands still clasped in each other's. Then Sylvie said, "Would you come in, Lena? If you have the time."

"Yes. I'd like that."

"I want to... to talk with you about something. If you –"

"Yes, whatever it is. Of course!" Lena let go of Sylvie's hand, and propped her bicycle against the hedge.

Sylvie nodded, and at last led the way down the path to her door.

"Would you come upstairs?" Sylvie asked in a hushed voice. When Lena did nothing but stare at her, she continued, "I don't mean anything –" Sylvie let out a soft sigh. "I just want to talk – privately. If you see what I –"

"Of course," Lena said, in quiet yet reassuring tones. And she followed Sylvie up the stairs to the safety of the first floor with no hesitation at all.

There was very little furniture up there. Still, it felt like a deliberate choice when Sylvie sat on the bed instead of anywhere else, swinging her legs up and shifting so her back was against the headboard. Lena climbed on, too, and settled cross-legged towards the foot of the bed, facing her friend but not too directly.

There was a pause before Sylvie finally confessed, "I haven't spoken about this to anyone. Other than Win. In great detail with Win! We talked about it – argued about it – endlessly. We were never going to agree." Sylvie grimaced as if the thought of it still caused her pain.

"I'm sorry," Lena offered. "Is this why you left London?"

"Yes. There were many reasons – not just the break with Win. It was a complicated knot – a tangle – that was never going to unravel. But this was the core of it."

Lena nodded, and didn't interrupt any further.

"We were suffragists – that's how we met. We followed Mrs Pankhurst – Emmeline Pankhurst. We were members of her Women's Social and Political Union. You must have read about all this in the papers."

Lena nodded again, though she couldn't claim to be hugely knowledgeable about 'The Woman Question', as it was referred to.

"Their goal is to gain the vote for women – by 'deeds, not words'. Violent protests. Prison terms and hunger strikes. Neither Win nor I went to prison," Sylvie added, at Lena's curious look. "But that's what we were part of. The newspapers dubbed us 'suffragettes'. They meant it as an insult, to belittle us – but Mrs Pankhurst took the term and made it our own. We took pride in it! And the Women's Union split away from the suffragists, who were committed to peaceful protests."

"Miss Perry," Lena surmised, thinking of her genteel appearance, "stayed with the suffragists?"

"No! No," Sylvie replied with a dry laugh. "A fair conclusion to make, having seen her – but no. Win broke as many windows and menaced as many policemen as any of us. She might look decorous, but she has a great throwing arm! It was the war, this awful war, that broke us apart. It was the war that drove me away from the Pankhursts and the Women's Union."

This all felt so new to Lena – even the context, let alone the specifics – that she could do nothing but sit there and wait for more.

"Do you remember? They said it would be over by Christmas," Sylvie continued. "Yet here we are, a year since war was declared, and no end in sight. I can't believe them anymore when they talk of it being over soon." She scoffed – and then bent her legs to pull them up closer to her chest, wrapping her arms around them as if needing the comfort. "Lena, I used to go to the hospitals in London to read to the men, the soldiers who had no one else to visit them. Their injuries! Horrific! And their experiences... Beyond anything I want to tell you." Sylvie paused, and then tentatively asked, "Your uncle...?"

"My Uncle Bill," Lena confirmed. "With the Post Office Rifles in France. He writes to us... always cheerfully." And she finally faced something that she'd probably always known at some deeper level. Whether Bill wanted to protect Lena and Ruth from the full truth of it, or his letters were censored – or both – he must be suffering and no doubt badly, too.

Sylvie said, "I'm sorry." After a few moments of sad reflection, she said, "I should backtrack. It's complicated!"

Lena nodded encouragement.

"We were working for women to be enfranchised. But even if successful, it's not as if the vote will be given to *all* women – just as it isn't given to all men. And I can promise you that when it finally happens, it will be given to a lot fewer women than men! They couldn't bear to be outnumbered. Or even to have equal numbers! There will be eligibility limits, and those will favour the few women who have least to complain about. It will hardly make any difference at all," she concluded.

"But as a first step...?"

Sylvie sighed. "Yes, perhaps. Yes, that's probably fair. *If* we can rely on them to take further steps in years to come. You're wise enough to know, Lena, that significant change comes in pieces; a jigsaw to be painstakingly constructed over years. More likely decades, in this case. With pieces lost along the way, and only some found again."

They sat there in silence, while Lena pondered the fact that she definitely wasn't wise enough to have guessed at this tale let alone to now foresee the crux of it.

"In the meantime," Sylvie eventually continued, "they welcome these few women into a system – a corrupt old system – that is sending thousands of our men to kill and be killed. Tens of thousands of men, women and children to suffer and die! Do we want to be part of that?"

Sylvie didn't wait for a response, but leaned forward and wrapped her arms tighter around herself. "Mrs Pankhurst's strategy when war was declared was to immediately call a halt to our protests. She thought that was the way forward for the Women's Union, for us to earn favour. To acquiesce to war and destruction – in return for a few paltry votes!"

And there it was. Lena curled in on herself, figuratively at least, to try to take all this in. She wasn't sure she entirely understood, but she would. She was sure of that. She would think about it, and talk about it with Sylvie, until she could follow and begin to anticipate every word.

In the silence, Sylvie had collapsed back against the headboard, and even shuffled down a little so she was half-lying on the bed – as if exhausted.

"This is," Lena ventured – "This is what has been weighing on your heart?"

"Yes," said Sylvie. "Thank you." She looked as vulnerable as a newly hatched bird. But she also looked grateful and even a little peaceful. "I wasn't sure, Lena, that anyone had even noticed that weight."

"This is the cause of your disagreement with Miss Perry?"

"Yes. She does not like the war, of course – but she thinks we must do our part and endure it. She continues loyal to the Pankhursts, mother and daughter, despite everything." Sylvie took a breath, and said, "There was almost a... purity to it at first. The Women's Union. Mrs Pankhurst and her family had worked with the Independent Labour Party, but she'd realised they weren't doing enough for women. So, when the Union started, we had no affiliations with *any* political party. And *now* we're... compromised beyond any affiliation we'd even imagined back then!"

Lena considered this, but had nothing relevant to say – or not yet. She returned to the previous matter. "Maybe, while Miss Perry is here, you can convince her. Or find common ground."

"No." Sylvie shook her head. "No, it's too important. It goes too deep, with both of us."

Lena nodded, though she wondered. Never having had a girlfriend herself, she wasn't sure about the kind of differences between individuals that such a relationship could survive. Surely *some* differences were necessary for a relationship to thrive! The two people forming a complementary set, rather than each being reduced so the pair could be made into one.

"*Now* what do you think about me living here?" Sylvie went on to ask. "They are right to suspect me. Do you see? My neighbours – your friends – are right to be suspicious. I *am* an outsider. I *am* against... how things are."

"I can see that better now," Lena agreed. She still had so much to think through. But the one thing she was certain of was that Sylvie meant no harm, not to anything or anyone Lena cared about.

Lena tipped forward onto her hands and

knees, and slowly crawled up the bed. Sylvie watched her, half wariness and half hope. At the last moment Sylvie shifted further so she was lying down, and reached out an arm so that Lena could cuddle in against her. They held on to each other for a lovely warm while.

Eventually Lena asked, "What do you think should happen? Should we be given the vote or not? And then what happens next?"

"There must be another way," Sylvie murmured, almost as if musing to herself. "I mean, *yes*, women should be enfranchised. But there must be a third way. *Many* other ways, beyond what I can imagine!"

Lena found herself clinging to Sylvie, dizzy with the possibilities.

"I cannot want to join what is being done now."

Sylvie seemed so sure of herself. Lena used to feel sure of herself, too. Now she wondered if that was because she'd just never asked enough questions or thought anything properly through.

"I love Britain and I love its people. I love Belgium and France and the whole world and its people! But I cannot love Parliament and I cannot love war."

They lay there together for a while, so comfortable. Lena felt a glimmer of wanting more, and even though she sensed Sylvie did, too, now wasn't the time. It was more important to share this safe haven in each other's arms.

"It all seemed so far away," Lena said.

"The war?"

"Yes. Until you came here." Lena shifted her head back so they could see each other's faces. "You must think we're... so out of touch."

Sylvie nodded at first, but then shrugged a little. "It's been nice in some ways. To remember that life continues. How long for, I don't know."

"How long until...?"

"Until the zeppelins find us. No, I know," Sylvie continued when she saw Lena's instinctive protest. "We're too far inland to worry about air strikes. But the war will catch up with us sooner or later. I am hoping later, but..." She grimaced in lieu of a shrug.

Lena sighed. Some of the light had gone out of the day. She squeezed Sylvie tighter for a moment, and then rolled away a little. One of her arms was going to sleep. But as she shook it back into feeling, she glanced out the window – and Lena realised that the dwindling light wasn't a metaphor. "Oh, *botheration*! I have to go, sorry." She hauled herself up off the bed, reluctant to leave Sylvie, of course – but she took her duties as postmistress too seriously to consider neglecting them. "The outgoing mail –" Lena paused in the doorway. "I have to get it ready. I'll be late!"

Sylvie was already up as well, and quickly followed her down the stairs. "Of course!"

"Not that my Mum can't do it," Lena explained over her shoulder, "but she has enough on her hands with the shop. I promised her I'd be there this evening."

"Can *I* help? You can take me on your bicycle. Or I'll catch up with you!"

That was worth another pause. Lena's heart thudded in gratitude, but she rose on her toes to press a kiss to Sylvie's mouth. "Not this time. Thank you. But another time." She hesitated, hoping Sylvie wouldn't mind the refusal, or not too much.

"Of course. Go! Go!" Sylvie waved her off from the front door, and Lena dashed away on the bicycle, swerving just far enough to throw Sylvie a grin and a wave.

All that evening and into the night, Lena's thoughts and feelings dwelt in that comfortable embrace they'd shared in the safest room of Sylvie's house. Lena had had doubts along the way, of course she had. She'd resisted such an enormous change in her life. But it was too late now – she was in too far – and she might as well just acknowledge as much.

Chapter Seven

When Lena and Sylvie arrived at Amy's for that afternoon's knitting group, they found Amy happily talking with Miss Perry. Lena held back for a moment to look down the hall into the kitchen, where Joe Martin was in quiet conversation with Mrs Doherty. She wondered if Joe was able to provide useful comfort or information about Fred Doherty's likely fate...

Before she could be caught intruding on them with her snooping, Lena followed the others into the sitting room. Amy settled Miss Perry by Sylvie, introduced her to the group, and then helped set her up with yarn and needles.

In the midst of which, Lena noticed that Sylvie had worn her necklace of glass beads again, and was now cradling the weight of it in one hand, while Miss Perry exchanged a delighted smile with her. It seemed that Amy noticed, too. "That's a lovely necklace, Miss Cawkwell. I meant to compliment you on it before."

"It was a present from a friend," said Sylvie.

"It's obvious you're very fond of it," Amy added, with a nod in Miss Perry's direction as well.

'*Yes, it's also obvious who her friend is,*' Lena grumbled to herself.

She had a smile for Joe when he came in to join them, though, sitting between Amy and Lena. Mrs Doherty settled on Miss Perry's other side, despite this not being her usual place, and her hands were soon busily occupied, and she kept her head low.

Through all of which, Miss Perry and Miss Cawkwell were looking at each other as if words had been stopped in their mouths, and they were each wondering whether the other would be brave enough to let them spill, or would mind very much if the other did so.

Eventually even Mrs Doherty noticed, and she shook her head in mild frustration. "No need to keep it under your hat, Win. My cousin and her friend," Mrs Doherty announced to the room at large, "are suffragists, and those beads are the movement's colours. Purple for loyalty and dignity –"

"White for purity," said Miss Perry, who was dressed appropriately.

"Green for hope," Sylvie concluded in satisfied tones.

There was a hush throughout the room as everyone took this in – or tried to. Then Gillian Wright said, very genuinely, "That is beautiful, ladies. Thank you." And the moment broke.

Soon everyone was industriously clicking and clacking and chatting away – except for Lena, who was still slow and clumsy... at knitting among other things. Her scarf had barely reached twelve inches long, and apparently needed to be five feet. She sighed. Probably rather loudly.

The room had fallen quiet, perhaps in deference to Mrs Doherty's situation, perhaps in confusion over whether suffragists could be approved of or not. Sylvie said, no doubt in an effort to divert attention, “Mr Martin, I’m pleased to see you’re looking well.”

Which he was, Lena noted. Even his jittery leg was no longer misbehaving.

“Thank you, Miss Cawkwell,” Joe responded.

“I hope this doesn’t mean you’ll be leaving us again soon?”

“No... No, they have me working on something here. Just office work for a few hours a week,” he added with a deliberate shrug.

“Oh, in town? Do you know, I have never once visited town since I moved here!”

Silence.

After a moment, Sylvie said with utmost sincerity, “I am so sorry. I didn’t mean to pry.”

Almost everyone in the room was bristling with suspicion again. It seemed that Sylvie was doomed to remain an outsider in the village. Miss Perry didn’t offer a riposte, but seemed a little resentful on behalf of her friend, a little impatient.

Joe’s bad leg shuddered once – but he said, easily enough, “Not in town, no. And no need to apologise, Miss Cawkwell. It’s just rare for anyone to be interested in bookkeeping! But I always said that bookkeeping would secure me a job anywhere – and I was right, wasn’t I, my love?” he added, turning to his wife.

“You were indeed,” she replied fondly.

By which time most people were concentrating on their knitting again. But Lena picked up what felt like a dropped stitch or two in some old ponderings. *Not in town...* Surely that must mean the old factory, which Lena had guessed was back in use despite it having been abandoned for years. Where else *could* Joe be working, in this village surrounded by fields and woods and not much else? Although if the factory were simply being used as a base to handle the village's excess vegetables and other produce, how much bookkeeping was actually required...?

Lena shook her head. No doubt the army was even fussier than the Post Office about numbers and sums and correctly completed forms, and the answer to her question was 'A *lot*.'

On the other hand... It was while walking Sylvie home that Lena was prompted to raise the matter with her again. "Do you smell that?" she asked. "When the wind's in the north..."

"There is something," Sylvie agreed after taking a couple of thoughtful breaths. "Something sharp... Almost... I'm not sure. Do you have wild garlic in the area?"

"I don't think so. Unless it's newly arrived."

Sylvie huffed a laugh, as if reflecting on how welcome new arrivals were. "It's very late in the year for garlic, anyway." A pause before she added, "Is someone pickling? It might be some kind of vinegar."

"Maybe," Lena agreed, feeling a sense of relief. The army could be preserving the vegetables they collected before shipping them out.

But Sylvie was continuing, "I'm not sure, though. The scent is... not quite right. Do you think? It's almost chemical, in a way! Unappetising, definitely."

Chemical. Lena's relief evaporated. Eva Rowan and her chemistry books – travelling to work in the same army truck as Joe Martin – heading in a direction mostly northward, from where this odd smell blew – where one could find an old laboratory building with a small landing strip –

Lena babbled all this at Sylvie, who seemed to understand at least the core concern if not the details: "You think something strange is going on?"

"Yes, I do. Oh, and the sheep are all gone – there's that, too!"

"But if it's army business..."

"It's not our business?" Lena sighed. "And the joke is on me if all they're doing is pickling cabbages! But what you were saying the other day... Isn't the war our business? Don't we get to have a say?"

Sylvie seemed deep in thought for a while, until they neared Fields Corner, where she paused with her hand on the garden gate. For a moment she considered Lena, with her brows knotted together in a frown. "You could take me for a hike. I used to love hiking, and this is such a pretty area."

The idea was like being struck by lightning. "You want to go see what they're up to?"

"Is it close enough? I could probably borrow a bicycle –"

"Better to go cross-country," Lena suggested. "They're more likely to be watching the roads. Aren't they?"

Sylvie nodded. "Do you have the time

available?"

"Friday afternoon should be all right," Lena said. "If that suits you. We want a weekday, I guess? I'll check with Mum about her doing the outgoing mail if I'm not back in time. I could ask Amy to help her, too."

Sylvie's eyes narrowed for a moment – but before Lena could react, Sylvie confirmed, "Friday afternoon it is, then."

"But what do you think you'll find there?" asked Emily, not bothering to muffle her exasperation.

"I don't know!" Lena replied. "That's the point!"

"It's the British Army, Lena. We're on their side, remember? Or at least, they're on our side."

"Meant to be, yes."

Emily was in her usual spot, half-sitting half-lying on the sofa with her hair loose over the back of it and her bare feet propped on the pouffe. "You honestly think that Joe Martin and Eva Rowan are up to no good?"

"They might not *want* to be."

"I wouldn't put anything past Eva Rowan," Emily acknowledged, "but Joe Martin is the kindest man in the village."

"They wouldn't have had a choice, would they!"

"Which is also my point."

Lena paused in her pacing, and puffed out a breath. "You can't claim my points as yours."

"The country is at war, Lena."

"A decision made by a bunch of old men in London. What's it to do with us?"

"Whether you personally agree with it or not, we're at war. And curiosity is dangerous enough at the best of times."

Lena stalked back and forth. "I want to know. Maybe I'm wrong!" she declared – loudly so it didn't sound like a concession.

It was Emily's turn to huff. "But what will it take for you to let this go? I mean, if you don't find anything, will you conclude that there's nothing to find? Or will you just assume you missed something and keep searching?"

Which was a fair point. No doubt Lena conveyed as much as her righteousness drained away. She walked over to the sofa, and sat down at a polite distance from Emily. They both indulged in some silent contemplation.

"You know what still puzzles me, darling?" Emily eventually asked.

"No." Could be any number of things. "What still puzzles you?"

"What happened to Eva Rowan's husband? He's been gone almost a year now – almost since before the war was even declared – and we've heard never a word from her about where or why."

"I always thought she knew, and that he was all right," Lena said – "or he's safe enough, anyway. She's never once seemed to mourn him."

"Hunt me down an answer to that, and I'll thank you." Emily smiled at her – one of her glowing smiles that lit up her eyes as well.

"Oh, sure," Lena complained. "*Now* who's

sticking their nose where it isn't wanted? What if he's, um... What if he's on a secret mission in France!"

"Sounds more exciting than staying home and growing cabbages."

"He must have thought so," Lena agreed.

"Let's hope he hasn't had reason to change his mind!"

And they both fell back into contemplation – more troubled than quiet this time.

Sylvie was dressed as usual in a shapeless dress and practical shoes – which was absolutely fine, as Lena was dressed as usual, too, in shirt, trousers and boots. "All set?" Lena asked as she propped her bicycle against the wall by Sylvie's front door.

"Yes. I packed supplies," Sylvie added, slinging a battered old satchel across her torso so that it hung by her hip.

"Supplies...?" Lena took a moment, but all she could think was, "For breaking and entering? For *spying*?"

Sylvie laughed. "For hiking! A flask of water, and some cheese, apples and biscuits, and a blanket for sitting on."

"Excellent," Lena said with a grin.

"I'm not sure how far we're walking, but I thought we'd better look the part, in case anyone questions us."

"So, I'm just showing you the lovely countryside hereabouts."

"And I'm walking for my health, which I

haven't done for too long."

"You need to get back into good habits!" Lena exclaimed.

"Exactly," said Sylvie. They shared a nod, and then Sylvie said, "You were planning to go cross-country?"

"Yes. Let's start from your garden." And Lena led the way around the back of the house and past the vegetable garden to where the long grasses climbed a short slope and then rolled into the beyond.

Once they had found a rhythm between them, setting a good steady pace that they could keep at all day, Lena introduced a topic she'd been curious about. "I'm being nosy..." she began.

"Yes?" Sylvie said, sounding just as curious as Lena.

"I couldn't help but notice... Well, I wasn't expecting Miss Perry to dress so differently to you."

Sylvie laughed under her breath. "I'm a great believer in Rational Dress, and in making my own clothes. It's not that Win doesn't agree... She never really took to corsets, and hasn't worn one for years."

Lena thought about Miss Perry's trim silhouette, and observed, "It's not as if she needs to!"

"She does have a good figure," Sylvie agreed. "The fashions of the day always suit her well – and her family can afford them." She paused for a moment's thought, before adding, "Win isn't as vain as you might expect for a woman so pretty."

"No, I didn't mean to criticise –"

"She simply is who she is, if you take my meaning. She has no pretensions."

"She's lovely," Lena agreed, heartfelt.

They were quiet for a while. Lena had steered them well, as they soon picked up a pathway that would take them around a particularly gnarly patch of forest. It was much easier walking an old trail instead of wading through the overgrown fields.

"It never even occurred to me to start wearing a corset," Lena continued eventually.

"I never wanted to either," Sylvie responded. "Not that I was considered strange or rebellious. My family was a lot humbler than Win's."

"You won't see many around here, anyway. Gillian Wright used to, but now it's just when she's in her Sunday clothes. Eva Rowan – you won't have met her yet, I don't think – Eva is the only one around here who regularly wears corsets... Don't ask me how I know!" Lena added with a laugh full of bravado.

Sylvie smiled at her fondly, as if it hadn't even occurred to her that being forgiven or unforgiven was relevant.

Lena judged that the time was right to strike out across the fields again. There were at least two thick hedgerows she knew of that would cut across their journey, but if she aimed well they could use the stiles to broach them.

"So," Sylvie said once they were back into their rhythm. "Eva Rowan...? There I was thinking that Mrs Martin must have been your first kiss."

"Oh!" Lena could actually feel her cheeks heat up. When was the last time she'd blushed? She couldn't remember at all. Maybe she never had. "Amy is..."

"Adorable," Sylvie supplied, still fond, with a touch of mischief.

"...the most adorable woman in the village. True. But my first kiss..."

"You don't have to tell me, Lena."

"...was Gillian Wright."

"An older woman!" Sylvie was obviously intrigued. "And married? Who was leading whom astray?"

Lena frowned over this for a moment. "Neither, I think. It was more as if... she was setting me on the right path."

Sylvie swerved in Lena's direction, and they instinctively slowed to a halt. "Then I'm very grateful to her," Sylvie said quietly, reaching to hold Lena's hand in hers. They leaned in closer to press a kiss to each other's lips. "I'm so glad I met you, Lena," Sylvie murmured.

Lena eased nearer, and took Sylvie's other hand. In between, their bodies were close enough to each feel the other's warmth. "I'm glad, too," she said.

They walked a while in silence, before Sylvie tentatively began, "The path that Mrs Wright set you on... Do you feel that it's definitely the path you want to follow?"

Lena cast her a puzzled look. "Yes. Do you

still need to ask?"

"Most women marry men anyway," Sylvie explained, "if they can – even if they are like us. Our society is organised that way."

"I didn't think you cared much about how society is organised!"

Sylvie nodded. "I've chosen to grow against the grain. But it's best to make it a choice. An informed decision."

"Well, consider me informed!" Lena declared happily. "Or decided, or something." After a moment's thought she added, "No, I've always gone my own way."

"Ploughed your own furrow?" Sylvie suggested with a quirk of her brow. They both burst out laughing.

Once they'd quieted again, Lena confessed, "I'm just not smart enough to think about it like you do. I don't have the words."

"That's all right," Sylvie said. "There's wisdom in your instincts, in being true to your nature, too."

Lena conveyed all her gratitude in a look.

Eventually, as they began making their way up a somewhat steeper rise than they'd encountered before, Lena slowed and said quietly, "If we're where I think we are, then we should have a good view of the old factory from up on this hill."

"So we should approach with caution."

Lena nodded – and as they neared the top of the slope, they both got to their hands and knees and crawled the last few yards. As she tentatively poked her head up, Lena saw that she hadn't led them astray. They were looking down at the rear of the main building, with a large shed and another small outbuilding off to the west – their left.

Everything was quiet, but a couple of parked army vehicles proved that Lena's suspicions had been right. "Ha!" she said in satisfaction, settling to lie on her front, propped up on both elbows.

Sylvie settled likewise, and exchanged a glance with Lena, amused but mostly impressed. "What do you think they're doing here?"

"*That* I have no idea about," Lena replied. "But they've been very secretive."

"Aren't they usually, though? Especially during wartime. They're not going to advertise their business to all and sundry."

"I suppose... But it's not as if we don't know where all the army barracks are. My Uncle Bill trained at Crowborough Camp in Sussex, and others did, too. And there's the London Home Depot, where they handle all the army's mail and telegrams –"

"– in Regents Park," Sylvie agreed. "I've seen it. A *huge* building." She paused for a moment before saying, "A lot of army bases are public knowledge, but that doesn't mean they *all* are."

Lena looked at her and grimaced. "All right, good point. But I still have to wonder..."

The two of them lay there staring down at the buildings. All remained quiet outside, and the few windows didn't provide even a hint of movement inside.

"Do they have guards stationed anywhere about?" Sylvie asked. "You'd think they'd have guards."

"If no one has even figured out they're here, though..."

"You did," Sylvie said – and this time there was no mistaking her obvious pride.

Lena smiled, feeling warmed through.

After a moment, Sylvie returned to the main topic. "I should have asked before: What was the factory originally used for? Does that give us a hint about what they're doing now?"

"Oh, they were making cloth – woollen cloth. We have so many sheep around here – *had* so many sheep."

"They were bringing the manufacturing closer to the source."

"Yes, but we're too far from anywhere. It only complicated the transport problems, having incoming supplies as well as outgoing produce. At least, that's what we were told."

"Was the landing strip meant to help solve that?"

Lena shrugged. "I was still in school when all this happened. I wasn't that interested!" She gazed at the overgrown corridor of grass that led off to the east. "I think they only put that in because the man who built the factory had a small plane that he liked to fly himself. Maybe if he hadn't been so used to flying about the countryside, he wouldn't have underestimated the transport problems!"

"That sounds fair." Sylvie paused thoughtfully. "So, spinning, weaving, and dyeing...

How would that relate to what they want the factory for now?" She looked around, before adding, "If I'd thought to ask about this before, I would have half expected to see your missing sheep."

"No, I think the army took them somewhere else entirely. I bet they were slaughtered for meat."

"Ah," said Sylvie – and then, under her breath, "*ah...*"

Lena saw the soldier a moment later, wandering along the back of the factory building.

"Don't move," Sylvie whispered.

"I won't." Not that the soldier was likely to glimpse the tops of their heads through the grasses on the hill above – he wasn't looking about him, even though he seemed to be on guard duty. A rifle was slung over one shoulder, and he was smoking a cigarette, his posture about as far from alert as possible. It seemed he'd long ago given up on expecting to run into trouble – or to have trouble run into him.

Once he'd taken a broad sweep around the level area surrounding the factory, he dropped the cigarette butt to the ground and trod on it, before making his way to the front of the building in a slightly better attempt at looking the part.

Lena and Sylvie collapsed limply to the grass, exchanged a glance, and both wriggled back down the slope a little way so they could safely sit up.

"Well!" said Sylvie – just as Lena exclaimed, "Right!" And then they both burst into muffled laughter, due to nervousness or relief or just plain silliness. "What seasoned spies we are," Sylvie concluded.

She reached for her satchel where she'd dropped it, and pulled out the flask of water – which she offered to Lena first, while Sylvie also brought out an apple each. Lena loved biting into the apple's crispness, and loved even more that Sylvie didn't bother wiping the flask's mouth before drinking herself.

They sat there in the grass in companionable silence until the apples were finished, and then Lena crept back up to peek over the top of the hill. "Nothing," she reported.

Sylvie was shaking out a small blanket and spreading it on the grass. "If we're supposed to be hiking for pleasure, we'd better act like it!"

"Fine by me," Lena said, stretching out to lie on her side, propped up on an elbow. She accepted the offer of another drink and a biscuit. "I like the way you do secret missions!"

A pleased look crossed Sylvie's face – and then she seemed to grow self-conscious for the first time that Lena could recall. "I also brought a book to read," she announced, producing a volume with a flourish.

Lena snickered, she couldn't help it, but then gathered herself to bluster, "I know I'm not great at conversation, but I didn't realise I was *that* boring!"

"Oh no, that's not it!" Sylvie blurted before subsiding. "You're teasing me," she said, with a return of the pleased expression. "I thought I'd read to you, in part because I know *I'm* that boring."

"Not even a little bit. What's the book?"

"It's a novel by George Gissing, called *The*

Odd Women. Do you know it?"

"No." Lena narrowed her eyes. "Why, should I? I'm not exactly a great reader."

"That's all right. I just thought you might – Well, it's about women like us, so I thought –"

"You thought we're odd?" A guffaw burst out of Lena, and became a slightly more civilised giggle.

"No... I mean, *yes*, in different ways – but it means the women who are left over. The ones who aren't paired off in marriage."

Lena could not contain her own mirth. "Why, because we're *odd*?" – conveying her meaning with a wink.

"That as well." Sylvie sighed impatiently – another first in Lena's experience. "May I make one serious point?"

"Please!" Lena replied, though by this time she was shuddering with helpless laughter. She wrapped her arms around her own torso in an effort to prevent herself cracking a rib.

"This is another reason why they don't want to give us the vote, do you see? There's this idea that we outnumber men, that there are a million or more 'surplus' women out there –"

"What, because of the war?" Lena asked, sobering abruptly.

"No – I mean, yes, I'm sure they think that's making it worse. But this book is ten or twelve years old. They were going on about this 'surplus' long before I moved to London and joined the suffragists."

Lena stared at her. "Is it true? That there's a million more of us than men?"

"I don't know," Sylvie replied. "It never would have occurred to me to think that, living in Yorkshire or in London. Even here, with only schoolboys and a few ancients in the village, I don't feel as if there aren't an equivalent number of men. It's just that they're somewhere else right now."

Lena pondered that – but honestly, thinking was about the last thing she felt like doing just then. She reached out a hand to Sylvie. "Come here, you odd creature!"

Now Sylvie chuckled, too, and she went willingly into Lena's arms. They kissed, and giggled, and rolled back and forth under the kind sunlight, with Sylvie's clumsy knees and elbows causing minimal damage. For those sweet moments all thoughts of hiking, spying, or picnicking seemed utterly irrelevant.

A horrid noise intruded, a familiar sound that didn't belong to such a beautiful day. Lena renewed their kiss and tried to ignore the interruption – but she couldn't. This was what they were here for.

"That rackety old truck," she muttered, pulling away from Sylvie's embrace and crawling back up to the top of the hill. "That never bodes well."

Sylvie crawled up beside her, and they watched a few soldiers loitering about the truck, with its tailgate open and waiting. Eventually a large pallet of brown-painted objects was wheeled out from the factory. The soldiers seemed to take great care in handling the load, which made Lena snort. It wasn't as if the truck or the local roads would make for a gentle ride!

"What are they exactly?" Sylvie whispered. "Can you make out any details?"

"It's definitely not pickles or preserves!"

"I'm afraid you're right."

"Tall cylinders... maybe two foot tall... metal, I think, though they're painted..." Lena pulled back in a moment's panic. "They're not pointed, but they wouldn't be missiles, would they? Or shells?"

"I don't know. Maybe. I'm not sure how aerodynamic they'd need to be. But there are munitions factories elsewhere. Enormous places. Why would they set up a small one here?"

"Something new? Experimental?"

They exchanged glances freighted with misgivings. Sylvie concluded, "Nothing good, then."

The two of them watched as the truck drove off with its cargo, and the remaining soldiers returned inside. After a while, it seemed that little else was likely to occur. Lena and Sylvie shifted back down the slope onto their blanket.

The sun was starting to lower in the sky. "We'd better head off," said Lena. "We don't want to be hiking cross-country in the dark."

"And the outgoing mail?" Sylvie asked, starting to pack up their picnic goods.

"Mum and Amy are taking care of it."

Sylvie shared a smile with Lena, and then crawled further down the hill before standing up to fold the blanket and stow it. They walked off together in silence, back the way they'd come.

Eventually Sylvie asked, "Do you want to

find out more about all this? Is there anything we *can* do, without tripping a wire? Metaphorically, I mean."

"I'm going to quiz Eva Rowan," Lena announced. "You can come, too, if you want. You should meet her, anyway."

"Not Joe Martin?"

"No, he's too nice. I don't want to put him on the spot or get him in trouble."

Sylvie laughed, as clear and musical as a bell. "But you don't mind interrogating Mrs Rowan?"

"Exactly," Lena agreed with a grin. "What are you doing on Sunday after church?"

Eva Rowan was as elaborately dressed and boldly made-up as she'd ever been. "Lena," she acknowledged when she opened the door to the pair of them. "And you must be the mysterious Miss Cawkwell of Fields Corner," Eva added, looking Sylvie up and down before offering her hand to shake.

"Pleased to meet you, Mrs Rowan," Sylvie responded, shaking Eva's hand. "Though I think you'll find I'm more prosaic than mysterious. Sorry if that disappoints you!"

"We'll see!" Eva narrowed her eyes at Sylvie, as if suspecting her of hidden depths and layers. After a moment, she turned away to lead them down to the dining room. "Come along, then. Are you staying? I was about to put the kettle on for tea."

"Sure," said Lena – before catching a

grimace and shrug from Sylvie. Uncertain how to interpret this, she raised her eyebrows in a query.

"Um... Mrs Rowan. Perhaps we should tell you why we're here first."

Which was a fair point, Lena thought. Eva might prefer to throw them out rather than offer hospitality.

Eva looked from one to the other with a flatly ironic expression. "I'm putting the kettle on anyway. I'll decide how many I'm making tea for later."

"Thank you," said Sylvie – and Lena led her in to sit at the dining table while Eva headed for the kitchen.

A moment later, Eva joined them, and stared at each of them again before demanding, "Tell me, then. Is this about the two of you?"

"What? No!" cried Lena in surprise. Though she couldn't help grinning when she saw Sylvie's cheeks were blooming red.

"She's already warned me off on your behalf," Eva mock-confided to Sylvie.

"Stop it!" Lena blurted. "We want to know what work you're doing – at the old factory, right?"

Eva sat back with her arms crossed and her face stony.

"Mrs Rowan," Sylvie said in even tones despite still blushing, "this is my fault. Please don't blame Lena. I had missed hiking since I moved here, and she kindly came with me to show me the country. We ended up at the factory quite by chance, thinking it was still abandoned –"

"No, we didn't," Lena interrupted. "We

meant to go there. I knew there was something strange going on."

"You're mad," Eva said. "We're at *war*, Lena."

"I know."

"Do you? You could go to prison for spying – or worse."

"You're making missiles there – that's worse than anything *I've* done!"

"Lena," Sylvie murmured, laying a gentle hand on her arm. "This won't get us anywhere."

Eva ignored her and declared, "What I may or may not be doing towards the war effort is absolutely none of your business, Lena."

"If it's *our* war then it's *our* business!"

"*Hopelessly* naïve," Eva muttered – before standing. "Get out, Lena. You, too, Miss Cawkwell of Fields Corner." This started sardonically, but ended with a half-amused huff. "Honestly, Lena," Eva continued as she saw them out the front door. "You do your war work – leave me to mine."

"What?!" Lena spluttered.

"It's about time you learnt to leave well enough alone!"

Lena struggled for appropriate words to aim at Eva – before feeling Sylvie's hand slip into hers, tugging her towards the gate. Running the Post Office wasn't war work... was it? Lena followed Sylvie readily enough, but couldn't help throwing a rebellious look back over her shoulder.

Eva taunted, "And be careful who you're friends with!"

Lena snarled – which she was sure Eva

would see and interpret correctly even if she didn't hear it.

And then Lena and Sylvie were walking back down the road, still hand-in-hand.

"I'll come to the shop with you, if that's all right, Lena. I haven't read a newspaper for far too long."

"What?" Lena had been silently stewing, and had to look around to work out where they were. It seemed Sylvie had already guided them in the direction of the village rather than back towards Fields Corner. "Oh. Yes, of course."

They continued on in silence for a while, before Sylvie ventured, "You were very angry with Mrs Rowan."

"We always argue! That's just how we are."

"She cares about you very much, then."

"No," Lena said with a frown. She grasped Sylvie's hand extra tight for a moment's reassurance. "No, she just likes having everything her own way. And keeping everything to herself. And that's fine, you know! Except when she's making missiles that have no other purpose than to kill people!"

Sylvie let a beat go by before saying, "You know I hate the war, Lena. But I find it hard to blame people such as Joe Martin, or Eva Rowan, or your Uncle Bill for doing what their country asks of them. Most people would say they've made the right choice."

"But *you* don't do more, do you? I mean... you said you read to the soldiers in hospital. But you didn't sign up to train as a nurse. Did you?"

"I didn't. Which was my choice. And most people would say I'm in the wrong."

Lena felt a fierce spark inside her. Was it a belated sense of patriotism? Was this how it felt for the men to get carried away and enlist, whether wisely or recklessly? "You know what I'd love to do? Drive ambulances. Or trucks."

"You're already doing plenty," Sylvie told her. "Running the Post Office. Helping your mother with the shop. Calling this the 'Home Front' isn't patronising or dismissive. We still need to run the country and take care of each other."

"Or I could go up to London and work in the big sorting office there. The Home Depot in – whichever park you said it was."

Sylvie looked at her searchingly for a long moment. They were reaching the outlying houses of the village, so they let go of each other's hand. Which wasn't great timing. Lena could have used the feeling of connection.

Sylvie repeated, "You really are doing good and useful work here, Lena. I don't think you need go looking elsewhere, unless you really want to."

"Are we hiding? We're such a long way from what's going on! Maybe we shouldn't... hide."

"Maybe," Sylvie agreed quietly. "But if that's our choice, that's all right, too."

"Is it?"

"Yes. A lot of people don't have the luxury of making that choice, but some of us do." Sylvie sighed, and examined Lena again before continuing. "The war breaks people, Lena. We can't let it break everyone. We need to make sure there's still a home left for our fighters to come back to."

Lena frowned, but didn't reply. She had too much to think about first.

The shop was closed, of course, this being Sunday. Lena led Sylvie around to the back door and showed her into the kitchen, before going to fetch a few recent newspapers which her mother had kept for wrapping up produce. "Here we are," Lena said, putting the papers on the table. "Take a seat. I'll make tea."

"Thank you, Lena." Sylvie hovered uncertainly. "Any chair?"

Lena pointed to the one where Bill used to sit before he enlisted. "Not that we're fussy about that kind of thing."

"You're not creatures of habit like the rest of us?"

"Oh well, I guess we are." Lena popped her head out into the hallway and called up the stairs. "Mum, are you here? I'm brewing a pot."

"I'll come down," Ruth replied.

"Sylvie's here," Lena added.

When Ruth entered the kitchen she smiled and said, "Lovely to see you, Miss Cawkwell."

"Thank you for having me, Mrs Pearce."

Lena belatedly realised this was the first time that Sylvie had visited any of the private parts of their home. Not that they were extensive, what with the shop, office and storeroom on the ground floor along with the kitchen, and the three bedrooms and a makeshift sitting room above.

"You'll stay for tea, I hope?" Ruth asked.

Sylvie glanced at Lena, who nodded encouragement. "I'd be delighted, thank you – but only if I won't be a burden."

"Of course not. We have bread baked fresh this morning."

"Thank you, that sounds wonderful."

And while Ruth started bustling around the kitchen, Sylvie's attention returned to the newspapers. Lena noticed, however, that she seemed lost in thought. After a few moments of silence, Lena said, "Sylvie. Did you find what you were looking for?"

Sylvie slowly looked up at her and eventually said, "No, but I've had an idea."

"Yes?"

"It's not exactly... a pleasant idea. Let me think about it some more."

"All right," Lena agreed. The kettle had boiled, so she filled the teapot.

Ruth asked, "Are you looking for work, Miss Cawkwell?"

"Oh, no... That is, I should look for work soon, if I'm staying, but that isn't why I was reading the newspapers."

"*If* you're staying...?" Lena blurted.

Sylvie smiled at her – fondly but not too fondly. As a friend would smile. "I agreed with Mrs Doherty to rent Fields Corner for six months. I wanted to leave London, but I wasn't sure if the country would suit me."

"And does it?"

The smile became genuinely happy. "Yes, it does. Though, as you remind me, Mrs Pearce, I can only live on my savings for so long."

Lena was just standing there staring at Sylvie, belatedly realising how much she'd come to rely on her company. The thought of Sylvie moving on stirred a belligerent turmoil in Lena's stomach. And yet here Lena was, hearing basic facts about Sylvie she could and should have learned long ago. Shouldn't she? Not that Lena ever wanted to be nosy, but it occurred to her that someone like Amy would have already discussed such matters with Sylvie in polite, friendly conversation weeks ago.

Ruth didn't let the silence drag on too long. "What sort of work would you be looking for?"

"I did clerical work in London. I most enjoyed working in a library, though I'm not qualified in any way; I was only an assistant. But I suppose that kind of work would only be available in town?"

"Probably, yes," Ruth agreed. "Though Joe Martin did well enough here in the village as a bookkeeper, before the war. He only went into town to work for one or two days a week."

Sylvie nodded. "I'd also be happy to try any kind of farmwork. I grew up in a rural area, very like this – though we only had a vegetable garden and chickens ourselves, so I don't have much direct experience other than helping with the harvest, but the life is familiar to me."

"I'm sure there are plenty of women here who'd be glad of an extra pair of hands on their farms."

Lena couldn't suppress a glint of humour at the thought of needy women wanting a hand. Sylvie caught her, but nodded solemnly for Ruth's sake.

"Let me know when you want to start work, and I'll keep an ear out for any opportunities," Ruth concluded, turning back to cutting the loaf of bread in economically thin slices.

Lena threw a wink and a grin at Sylvie, who responded with a shake of her head – and a barely concealed smirk.

Chapter Eight

As usual, the knitting group met at Gillian Wright's on the Tuesday afternoon. What was unusual was that Joe Martin attended as well; he had so far only joined them on Thursdays when the group met at Amy's and his home.

"It's nice to see you, Mr Martin," said Sylvie. "I hope you're well." Somehow she hit exactly the right note of concern for a friend and a lack of interest in his work.

"Yes, thank you," he replied in relatively muted tones. "Excused from duties today."

"I'm glad," Sylvie acknowledged as she walked past him into Gillian's sitting room.

The others had already shuffled around the chairs so that Joe could sit in his usual place between Amy and Lena. Mrs Doherty and Miss Perry sat on the other side of Sylvie. After everyone had settled, their corner of the room fell into quiet productivity while the rest of the attendees chatted.

Quiet productivity except for Lena, of course. "It's not that I don't *want* a deserving solider to wear this scarf," she announced, "but I'm beginning to think the war will be over before I am finished knitting."

There were various huffs of mild amusement. "That would be a fine thing," murmured Amy, eyeing the length so far. Lena's scarf was maybe half complete by now. She tried stretching it out to make it look longer, but Sylvie gave her a scolding look.

"None of that!" Sylvie cried. And in gentler tones, "You'll get quicker as you gain confidence."

Joe just watched her progress for a while, as if lost in his own thoughts. Which was enough to make Lena self-conscious – and she dropped the next stitch. "Whoa!" she cried – and she quickly stabbed her righthand needle through the crucial loop before it could run very far down the ladder of rows.

"Well done!" cried Joe. "Now, do you know how to repair that?"

"Not yet. Do you?"

"Not yet! Miss Cawkwell, can you show us?"

"Of course. It's easiest with a crochet needle..." Sylvie dug around in her bag and produced a short needle with a hook on the end.

Lena sighed. "What's that...? Crow-shay? I am so confused..."

"That's all right," Sylvie said. "Just watch for now, and even it doesn't make sense today, at some stage it will all snap into place."

Sylvie proceeded to demonstrate how she picked up the stitch, and climbed back up the ladder of rows with it. Which was lost on Lena – and maybe lost on Joe, too, for he seemed to be paying more attention to Lena and Sylvie than he was to learning new skills.

Joe continued to seem distracted for the rest of the afternoon, and then made a point of waving farewell as Sylvie and Lena walked down Gillian's front path.

"Can I come help you with the outgoing

mail?" Sylvie asked Lena. "Or keep you company, at least?"

"Sure," said Lena. Sylvie set a quick pace as she strode off in the direction of the village. "Is something wrong?" Lena asked as she hurried to catch up.

"He knows. Joe Martin knows. That we went to the factory. That we confronted Mrs Rowan."

Lena frowned. "I always thought Joe and Eva were unlikely friends, but –"

"Do you think that explains it?" asked Sylvie. "Or do you think it's more widely known?"

"Oh. Well, I hope the first."

"So do I."

They walked on for a while, before Lena at last said, "You never did tell me what your idea was – about what they're doing at the old factory?"

Sylvie shook her head, looking troubled. "It's not that I don't want to tell you – but I'd rather raise it with Mrs Rowan directly."

"I'll come with you," said Lena. She didn't quite make it a question about whether she was welcome to or not.

"We'll have to try talking with her, though, rather than arguing."

"I can do that." Lena repeated it as a promise: "I can do that."

"You two again!" Eva Rowan exclaimed, finding Lena and Sylvie on her doorstep that evening.

"I'm sorry, Mrs Rowan," said Sylvie, "but I have concerns I wish to share with you."

Eva stared hard at Sylvie. "This is wartime, Miss Cawkwell. If you have concerns about Lena, I can assure you that's none of my business. Any other concerns relating to me are none of *your* business."

"It occurred to me," Sylvie said very steadily, "that you are helping to make tear gas – or worse – at that factory."

For a moment Eva stood there like granite. But then the faintest crack showed in her expression. "You are really going to insist on talking about this?" she ground out.

"I'm sorry, Mrs Rowan," Sylvie repeated, "but –"

Eva took a step back, and with a jerky gesture invited them inside. Sylvie and Lena slid in and headed down to the dining room. None of them sat down.

"The use of tear gas is not a violation of the Hague Treaty," announced Eva. Her voice shook.

"No," Sylvie gently agreed, "but poisonous gases are. Such as the chlorine gas used by the Germans near Ypres."

Eva did not respond. Lena felt her knees go weak – for the wrong reasons – and sat down at the table. The other two followed suit.

Sylvie continued very carefully, "It seems reasonable to assume – ghastly though the idea is – that we are at least researching ways of using the same type of weapon. That we would deploy it as soon as we could usefully counterattack."

"This really is," Eva replied, her arms folded across her chest and her posture hunched as if she were cold, "absolutely none of your business."

Eva Rowan had never been anything other than cool, calm and confident. Now the cold she seemed to feel found an icy echo in Lena's own gut. "Eva," Lena said hoarsely. "Is that really what you're working on?"

"Is what I'm doing here any worse than what your uncle's doing over there, Lena? Killing. Maiming. Bringing misery – and not just to those directly involved."

Lena didn't have an answer.

"What if something goes wrong at the factory?" Sylvie asked. "They moved the sheep away for the sake of safety, didn't they? They wanted to protect that resource. But what about the people here? Your friends, your family – your lovers."

"*That's* what happened to the sheep!" cried Lena in shock.

Eva twisted her mouth in a grimace and didn't deign to respond.

"The Hague Treaty makes it clear that this kind of warfare is a crime," said Sylvie – still gently yet firmly.

Eva stared at her for a long moment. "The army – No, the British *government* has decided to retaliate against Germany with equal and opposite force – Who am I to deny my duty to serve my country?"

"You are someone who knows more than most what the effects are. You are someone who knows what actions are considered to be war crimes." Sylvie took a breath. "Saying 'they did it first' isn't a moral defence, even when it's true."

Eva stood up. "Get out, both of you."

Sylvie persisted. "Mrs Rowan, if there's anything we can do to help you –"

Lena belatedly came up with a theory of her own. "Is this because of your husband, Eva? Did you find out what happened to Lee?"

"Get out!" Eva was furious – but she had tears running down her cheeks as well. She was grieving. "Both of you. Now."

"I'm sorry," said Sylvie quietly, before leading the way back to the front door.

"*Eva,*" Lena murmured heartfelt as she passed her by –

But Eva just shook her head. No, she didn't want their help, their attempted comfort. Their presence.

A moment later the door was closed and locked, and Sylvie and Lena were walking down the road hand-in-hand.

Sylvie seemed shaken. Humbled. "I'm not sure anymore what I hoped to achieve," she said quietly. "All I did was anger her, upset her."

"I did that, too. I shouldn't have brought up her husband. But it just suddenly made sense. Sort of."

Sylvie looked across at Lena. "What happened to her husband?"

"Well, he's been missing. Pretty much since the beginning of the war. But none of us know what happened or where he was."

"Mrs Rowan hasn't talked about it?"

"Not to anyone. He was... They're both super-intelligent. And what with all the secrecy, I guess I was thinking he might have been a spy, and got caught in Belgium or Germany, or something like that."

"And then you thought, this evening, that she might want to avenge him."

Lena shrugged awkwardly. "Maybe?"

Sylvie nodded, and seemed to be contemplating this.

"But what about the sheep!" Lena exclaimed. "Speaking of super-intelligent! How did you come up with that?"

"It's only a theory..."

"No, I'm impressed." Lena shook their clasped hands. "You're far too smart for me, you know."

Sylvie smiled at her. "I'm not sure about that – but I do think we have enough common ground to stand on, you and I."

Lena laughed. "Is that the secret? It's not as if..." She took a breath. "I've never had a real relationship, you know? I didn't think I ever would."

"It's not a secret so much as another theory," Sylvie replied. "Enough common ground to be comfortable together, to understand each other – and enough differences to learn from each other, to keep it interesting."

Nothing to argue with there! Lena nodded. "That sounds good."

They had found their way – with no real intent on Lena's part – to Fields Corner, and they came to a stop by the gate, shifting around to face each other. There was a moment in which they didn't kiss, but Lena was certain they were both thinking about it.

Eventually Sylvie said, "Would you like to come in? I can offer you... fresh tea and a biscuit that is probably a bit stale by now."

"Sounds perfect," said Lena.

They sat cater-corner at the kitchen table, and they drank their tea. Dusk fell, and they sat there still, silent as if caught in a web. When it finally became dark, Sylvie rose, and lit the remaining half of a candle waiting in a holder. She held her free hand out to Lena, and tilted her head towards the staircase, asking the question. Lena nodded. *Yes.*

Sylvie led the way, the candlelight flickering and dappling their feet and calves as they climbed. Then they were in the bedroom, and Sylvie placed the candleholder on the wooden chair that served as bedside table. And Sylvie began divesting herself of her clothes.

Lena's hands lifted to the buttons of her own shirt – but then she paused. Naked... in a bed... She cleared her throat, and confessed, "Some of this is new to me."

"If there's anything –" Sylvie had paused, too. "Just tell me."

"No, it's just... Never mind. I can be brave."

"The bravest woman I know," Sylvie insisted. She was down to her slip, a cotton garment as shapeless as her dresses. "I'm sorry I'm not... very appealing."

"You have the most beautiful throat I've ever

seen," said Lena. "All long and elegant." She was down to her pants and socks now. She'd never needed a brassiere. "It's not like I'm all delicious womanly curves, anyway!"

"I've never minded a tomboy figure..."

"I like you, Sylvie. The way you are, who you are. I'd like you even if you *didn't* have a swan's neck!"

Sylvie shivered a little, possibly due to the night's slight chill. "Come to bed, then," she invited, pulling back the covers.

Within moments they had discarded the last of their clothes, and Lena climbed into the three-quarter bed, into Sylvie's arms... The touch of flesh against flesh from top to toe made her gasp. And then Sylvie pushed in closer still to kiss her.

For a long while the holding and the kissing were *everything*. Bodies shifting against each other, hands stroking and exploring. Their early awkwardness had vanished within moments, and instead they each simply *enjoyed* the other. Blessed the other and were blessed, giving, always giving.

Lena's hunger built and built, until at last her body was demanding fulfilment. She groaned needily as Sylvie's mouth explored her collarbone, pushing and rubbing herself against Sylvie's broad thigh.

"Here," Sylvie murmured. "Here... Let me do this for you." And her fingertips delved into dampness, strummed across Lena's nub and then plucked out exquisite notes of pleasure. Lena arched and thrust as the ultimate waves shuddered through her.

She clung to Sylvie, pressing her tenderness, her sensitivities close as the quakes finally quietened. And then it was a gift, an honour to do the same for her friend in return.

Chapter Nine

Lena was walking her bicycle and Sylvie was leading Christabel from Mrs Doherty's to Fields Corner the next evening, when the ground quaked and it sounded as if the sky were rent apart. A wind buffeted at their backs for a moment – and when they'd regained their balance, they turned to see a filthy column of smoke rising, underlit by what must be flames.

They stared for a long moment, endeavouring to comprehend.

"A zeppelin found us?" Sylvie choked out.

Lena instinctively added up the direction and the distance. "It's the factory!" She had already swung her leg over to mount the bicycle, and grasped the handlebars – but she paused to shoot a querying look at Sylvie.

"Go!" Sylvie cried.

She pushed off, lent in, and pedalled fiercely up the road. Within minutes an army truck careered in her direction, but passed her safely, perhaps not even realising she was there. Then a car overtook her, tooting its horn to warn her – someone shouted out the passenger window at her, but they were gone a moment later and she hadn't understood. She looked around when she could, but didn't glimpse anything in the dusk sky that might have been a zeppelin. Surely they were huge, and not the sort of thing you'd overlook...?

Lena finally reached the road's last crest, and

stood on her pedals to glide down the slope.

The factory was on fire – the *ruin* of the factory was on fire – with smoke pouring up from flames and jagged metal, with broken bricks scattered around, and glass shattering in the heat. Soldiers were aiming two firehoses at the blaze, but the water had no discernible effect. Others stood by, unable to do anything but wait.

Lena pulled up by the side of the nearest solider. He had on a gasmask. "Was anyone inside?" she asked, pitching her voice to carry over the infernal noise.

He shook his head, and gestured to his ear, indicating he hadn't heard. They were all wearing gasmasks.

"Was anyone inside?" she shouted. But she already knew the answer. There were no civilians to be seen. No Eva. No Joe.

The soldier turned and beckoned her to walk with him, further away from the fire.

Eva would have waited until Joe was safely home with Amy.

"You don't want to be here, Miss," he shouted – and she understood, despite his mask.

There was an acrid smell in the air. It caught in Lena's throat. Someone was trotting towards her with a spare mask in hand. "My friend – Eva Rowan – *was she inside*?"

"You *don't* want to be here, Miss!" It was an order.

She found herself coughing and her eyes were tearing up. And there was nothing she could do there. Nothing she could do now. But what had she done?

God, what had she done?

Lena waved away the offered gasmask, and set her foot on the pedal. Another brief coughing fit, and then she was making her way back up the road.

By the time she'd crested that rise, the air was clear again, and she filled her lungs with it – before leaning in and dashing as fast as she could towards Amy's house.

Lena was not surprised to find Sylvie there already. "He's all right," Sylvie said, coming down the path towards Lena as soon as she pulled up. "Joe's here and he's all right."

They clung to each other for a moment in relief, before Lena pulled back a little and said, "I don't think Eva is, though. I think we've lost Eva."

Sylvie nodded solemnly, and they made their way inside. Joe met them, his face ghostly white – and Lena hugged him for the first time in her life, and then hugged Amy, too.

Amy was feeding their children tea in the kitchen, so the other three adults retreated to the sitting room for the sake of discretion. As if any child in England could remain innocent during this war.

"She destroyed it, didn't she?" Lena asked. "Eva blew it up."

Joe didn't say anything but nodded.

"And herself."

"Yes," he said. "At least... I don't know for sure – I spoke with her this morning – not that she said anything clearly, of course, nothing that I understood at the time – but I *know* now."

Lena and Sylvie understood exactly what he meant.

"It was my fault," Sylvie said quietly. "I confronted her –"

"It was *my* fault," Lena interrupted.

"It was an accident," Joe said, overriding them.

"What?" Lena blurted, trying to take in this sudden course change. Did Joe *mean* it?

"For her sake and my sake – and for your sake, too, both of you – it was an accident."

"Oh." It wasn't that Lena had gone too far down the wrong track. A cover story. Or, more to the point, a pretence of ignorance.

"Of course," said Sylvie.

Lena only realised that she and Sylvie were sitting close together and clasping hands when Amy came in, and they instinctively parted.

"Don't worry," Amy murmured in their direction – and then she said to Joe, "Would you mind bathing the kids tonight?"

"Of course," Joe replied, getting up, and nodding a farewell to Lena and Sylvie before leaving the room. They heard him talking with the children, his voice almost cheerful and definitely loving.

Amy sank into the armchair he'd vacated, and slid down to rest her head on the back. After a moment's contemplation, she looked across at her companions. "He'll be fine," she said, as if reassuring herself as much as them. "We have such blessings in our life together. It's good to be reminded of that, every now and then, and feel grateful."

Sylvie murmured, "Gratitude, yes."

Amy offered them a small yet genuine smile. "*You're* both well," she said. "And happy?"

She meant... Amy meant everything about Lena and Sylvie, Sylvie and Lena. The odd women who had made a pair. Amy knew and wished them joy.

"Yes," said Lena, from her heart and her gut.

"Very happy indeed," said Sylvie.

Their hands reconnected with each other, and Amy's smile grew. "I'm so glad."

Chapter Ten

The funeral was delayed for a week, because the army took their time releasing Eva's body. '*Or what's left of it,*' Lena always silently added to herself whenever the subject arose. She tried to only remember Eva alive – preened and painted, but also brilliant and lusty – and she tried very hard not to imagine the little that remained.

Still, they were at war, and some friends and families were left with even less to mourn over – sometimes only words on a telegram. *Missing in Action Presumed Dead.* At least Eva's friends were left with no uncertainty about her fate.

While they were waiting – and with Gillian Wright's encouragement – Lena and Sylvie located Eva's diary and address book at her house, and worked out which solicitor in town she'd patronised. Lena used the Post Office telephone to call him, and discovered that the army had already informed him of what had happened.

Lena frowned, trying to work this out. "You mean, she gave them your details when she was recruited?"

"Yes. In effect, she nominated me – or this firm, in my absence – as next of kin."

"Well, that's..." Lena exchanged a confused look with Sylvie. "No! What about her husband?"

The solicitor sounded sympathetic. "I realise little information has been made available publicly, but I can confirm I hold a death certificate for

Henry Lee Rowan."

"From when? Where?"

"Mr Rowan died in September 1914. I'm afraid that's all I can tell you – though I can add that Mrs Rowan's last will and testament was signed in October."

Lena sat there in silence for a long moment, trying to remember if Eva had ever mentioned any other relatives. Eventually she said, "I can't think of anyone else –"

"That's all right," the solicitor assured her. "I'm certain that Mrs Rowan would have appreciated your involvement in helping plan her funeral. The village rector will know what to do. And then we can organise the reading of the will. There's no great urgency, Miss Pearce, but I trust you will attend."

"All right," she replied vaguely. "If I can bring a friend," she added, thinking of Ruth or Gillian, who had much more experience with this kind of thing – and thinking of Sylvie, too.

"Of course," the solicitor replied, and then they ended the conversation with thanks and farewells.

Lena once again turned a confused expression towards Sylvie. "Apparently I'm to be there when Eva's will is read. Does that mean it's read out loud? Is that a legal part of the process or something?"

Sylvie nodded in reply, and added, "Perhaps she left you something."

Finally the funeral service was held, and attended by everyone in the village who was able to. Eva Rowan had kept herself to herself, and had no very close friends, but she was still part of the community – and Lena suspected that the drama of Eva's death encouraged people's curiosity if their piety was lacking.

The rector had asked Lena to read aloud from the Bible, suggesting various passages about offerings and sacrifice. Some she thought were just downright strange or inappropriate. "Does he really want," she said to Sylvie and Ruth over the Pearces' kitchen table, "to compare Eva to Jesus Christ? Even Eva would think that was over-egging the pudding. And there's this weird bit about a sacrifice with 'a sweet-smelling savour'..."

Later that evening she confided to Sylvie, "One of those passages went on about fornication and filthiness, too. I don't know if that's the rector's way of undermining Eva's reputation, but I'm not going to play along."

"Quite right," said Sylvie.

"I'll do the one about charity," Lena told the rector. He sighed, no doubt thinking it had already been done a few times too many, but he didn't argue.

So she read from Ruth's copy of the King James Bible, taking the liberty of changing the tongue-twisting '-eth' words. "*And though I have the gift of prophecy, and understand all mysteries and all knowledge, and though I have all faith so that I could move mountains – and have not charity – I am nothing.*

"And though I bestow all my goods to feed the poor, and though I give my body to be burned – and have not charity – it profits me nothing.

"Charity suffers long, and is kind; charity envies not..."

After they'd laid Eva to rest in the churchyard, Sylvie asked quietly, "Did Mrs Rowan have charity, then?"

"She had something!" Lena declared. "And whatever it was, maybe the rest of us need more."

Lena was stunned. "She left me *everything.*"

Emily nodded at Lena from her usual place reclined on the sofa. "That was a surprise to you?"

"Yes!" Lena stared hard at her friend. "Isn't it to you?"

"Yes, but it makes sense."

"Does it? The house and everything in it. A bank account and shares." Lena wasn't even sure what shares were exactly, but she knew well enough that they were valuable. "This is *awful.*"

"Once Eva knew for sure that she'd lost her husband – and if there was no other family – then why not?"

"But I mean..." It got worse the more Lena thought about it. "Did *everyone* know? Oh hell, the things I've said this past week. About her charity and such. People will think I had expectations – Maybe people will even think –"

"What do you care what people think?" Emily asked with a slight scoffing tone.

"Putting myself forward as if I were chief

mourner, when I was just trying to do right by a friend…"

"If people think otherwise, that's their problem. It's not as if anyone else in the village went out of their way to support her."

Lena shook her head – then shook her whole self, as if she could get the sense of it all to finally settle into place. "I can't even say I was a friend to her! Not a real one. We argued as often as not."

"Darling," said Emily, "you'll just have to accept it: you were of more use to her than everyone else in this village added up together. Both practically and emotionally. And she has repaid you in kind."

"She has?"

"Yes." Emily sat up straight at last, as if wanting to emphasise her point. "Eva Rowan has given you *freedom*."

"I'll still be here every weekday and Saturday to run the Post Office," Lena anxiously assured Ruth, "and I'll help with the shop as much as I always have."

"I know, Lena," said Ruth. "And we'll still have dinner together at midday. On Sundays, too, if you like. You're always welcome, too, Miss Cawkwell."

"That's very kind of you, Mrs Pearce."

Lena nodded. The three of them were sitting around the Pearces' kitchen table, dealing with a greater change than Lena had ever expected. Greater even than the war, when she thought only of her own circumstances. Lena was only now realising that she had always loved her life, that she'd assumed it would never change, that she would live her whole life in this house, sleep every night in the same familiar bedroom.

But now she was moving out into a home of her own.

The conversation had stalled, until Sylvie offered, "I'll be able to help, too, with both the Post Office and the shop. Well, you'll have to teach me, of course, but I'd be happy to support you both."

"You have work of your own now, Miss Cawkwell. Don't let us try to claim time you can't spare!"

"I won't be working full-time, though. Joe will still be here two days a week, at least."

With the factory gone, the army had transferred Joe Martin to a staff position at the nearest training base, less than an hour's train-ride away from town. They were all selfishly relieved that his ongoing rehabilitation would keep him in Britain, for the foreseeable future at least. And Joe had asked Sylvie to help him restore and run his bookkeeping business.

"Will you be all right," Lena asked her mother, "sleeping here alone?"

"I'll be fine, Lena. We have good neighbours – and it's only until your uncle comes home, anyway!" Ruth paused, and looked at Lena softly yet very directly. "What about you?" she asked. "Such a distance from the village, too."

Lena returned her look, and felt her cheeks colour. *She knows. She probably knows everything, though I never told her.* "I won't be alone, though," Lena finally replied. "I'll have my best friend with me."

Ruth looked from one to the other of them – and suddenly she blinked, almost winced, as if tears were pricking at her eyes. Tears of happiness, though, for then she smiled. "Lena, Miss Cawkwell – or may I call you Sylvie? It's such a lovely name."

"Thank you," Sylvie replied, also damp-eyed. "I'd be delighted."

"I'll be grateful knowing you're there together, taking good care of each other."

Lena got up and walked round the table so she could lean in and wrap her mother in the tightest hug of all.

"I've been thinking about what to do with Eva's science texts," Sylvie announced one day as they were clearing tea from their very own dining table.

"You mean, other than reading them?" Lena asked.

Sylvie laughed. "Oh, most of them would be far beyond me. Especially the chemistry books!"

"No use me even trying, then!" They regrouped in the kitchen, and Lena filled the kettle to heat water for washing up.

"Always selling yourself short, Lena! One day you're going to surprise yourself."

Lena fondly shrugged this off. "Not in relation to science, anyway!"

"Are any of the young people in the village heading for university? Any of the children particularly clever?"

"It's no use asking me! I never had the knack for getting along with kids."

Sylvie didn't seem to mind this dire confession of Lena's. "We can ask Amy or Gillian, then," Sylvie continued without a pause. "But if there's no one in particular at present, we can still ensure people have access to them."

"Yes...?" Lena poured the hot water into a tub in the sink, added soap, and started washing the crockery.

"We can donate them to the town library, as the 'Eva Rowan Collection'. Then anyone who needs them can benefit."

"I love it," said Lena, leaning across to press a kiss to Sylvie's cheek. The wash-water got sloshed onto a freshly dried plate in the process, but Sylvie sorted that without complaint. "All your books, though..." Lena mused. "Your 'Odd Women Collection'."

"Yes?" Sylvie paused. "My suffragist and feminist texts...?"

"They're staying right here with us. Anyone who loves you, has to love your books, too – that's the deal."

Sylvie considered this for a long moment, before tentatively suggesting, "We might lend a volume or two out, though, as the need arises...? For the greater good, you understand."

"For the greater good," Lena agreed with a grin.

❖

About the Author

Ordinary people are extraordinary. We can all aspire to decency, generosity, respect, honesty – and the power of love (all kinds of love!) can help us grow into our best selves.

I write stories about 'ordinary' people finding their answers in themselves and each other. I write about friends and lovers, and the families we create for ourselves. I explore the depth and the meaning, the fun and the possibilities, in 'everyday' experiences and relationships. I believe that embodying these things is how we can live our lives more fully.

Creative works help us each find our own clarity and our own joy. Readers bring their hearts and souls to reading, just as authors bring their hearts and souls to writing – and together we make a whole.

I read books, lots of books, and watch films and television. I admire art, and love theatre and music. I try to be an awesome cog in the wheel of the world. I live an engaged and examined life. And I strive to write as honestly as I can.

I have lived in two countries – England and Australia – and travelled as well. I love learning, and have completed courses in all kinds of things. My careers have been in Human Resources, and in eLearning and training, so there has always been a focus on my fellow human beings and on understanding, conveying, sharing information.

Knitting gives me some down time and the chance to craft something with my hands. Coffee gives me stimulation and a certain street cred. My favourite colour is a green-blue teal.

I think John Keats is the best person who has ever lived.

And that's me!

Julie Bozza. Quirky. Queer. Sincere.
juliebozza.com

Titles by Julie Bozza

The Butterfly Hunter Trilogy:
Butterfly Hunter
Of Dreams and Ceremonies
Like Leaves to a Tree (story)
The Thousand Smiles of Nicholas Goring

Novels and Novellas:
The Apothecary's Garden
The Definitive Albert J. Sterne
The Fine Point of His Soul
Homosapien ... a fantasy about pro wrestling
Mitch Rebecki Gets a Life
A Night with the Knight of the Burning Pestle
A Threefold Cord
The 'True Love' Solution
The Valley of the Shadow of Death
Writ in Blood

Stories and Anthologies:
Call to Arms
A Certain Persuasion
Clarity
Crisis at Christmas & Christmas Present
A Death in Tombstone, A.T.
An English Heaven
Geek Elders Speak
Heroines
Love in Every Stitch
No Holds Bard

No Man's Land
A Pride of Poppies
Queer Weird West Tales
Rock Paper Water
We Live Without a Future
Wyngraf

Translations:
Chasseur de papillons (French)
La cérémonie (French)
Les mille sourires de Nicholas Goring (French)
Nous (French)
Jäger des verlorenen Schmetterlings (German)

www.ingramcontent.com/pod-product-compliance
Lightning Source LLC
Chambersburg PA
CBHW030935060726
47591CB00005B/1812
* 9 7 8 1 9 2 5 8 6 9 4 3 9 *